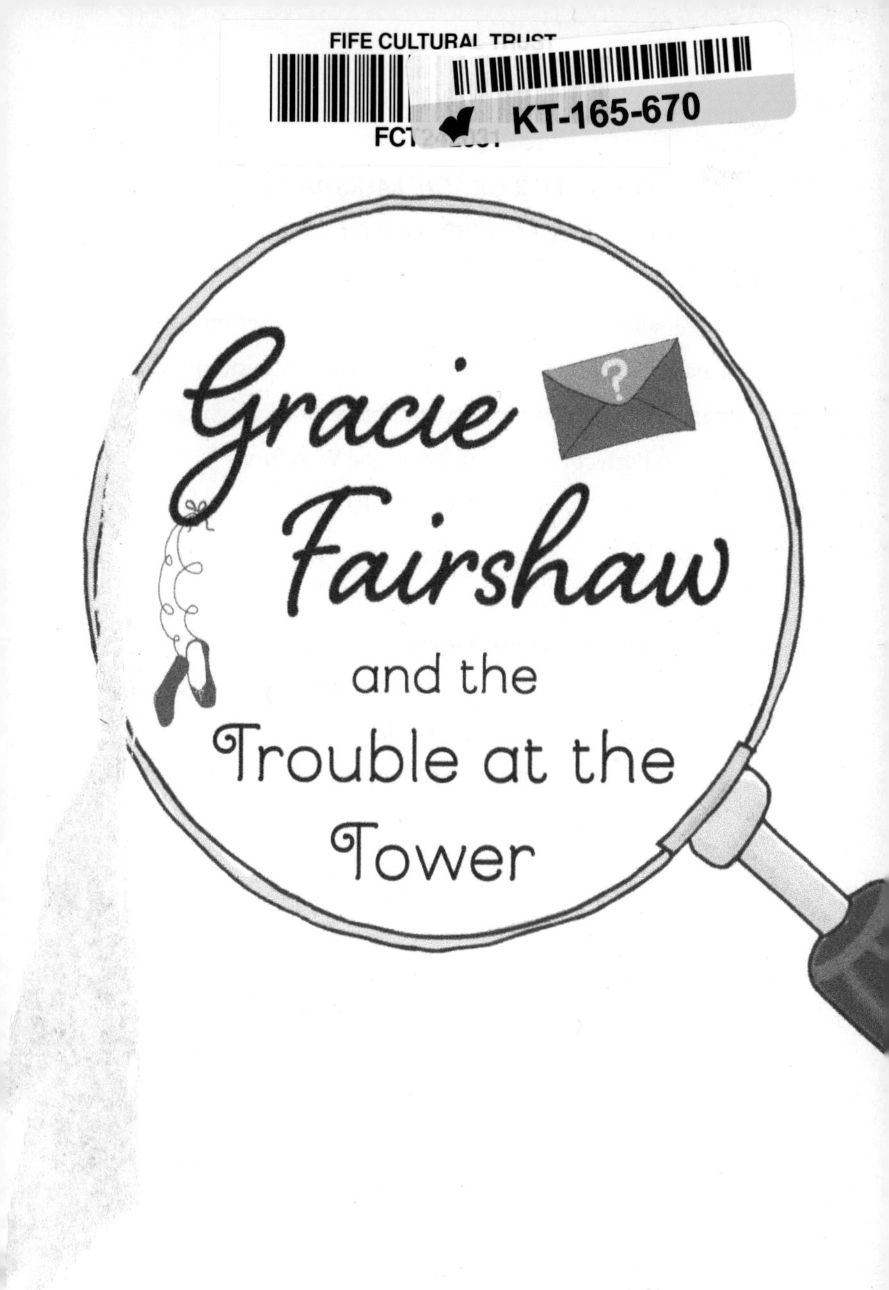
Gracie
Fairshaw
and the
Trouble at the
Tower

PRAISE FOR *GRACIE FAIRSHAW AND THE MYSTERIOUS GUEST*:

'*Gracie Fairshaw and the Mysterious Guest* is an exciting, fun and fast-paced adventure, crammed with mystery, unforgettable characters and more than a little bit of Blackpool magic. Perfect for fans of Katherine Woodfine.'

ANNA MAINWARING

'Brownrigg's love of Blackpool's seaside heyday shines brightly from every page. A book sure to switch on and illuminate every child's love of reading.'

BARBARA HENDERSON

'Meticulously researched and sprinkled with just the right amount of nostalgia, Brownrigg conjures up the perfect setting for this traditional crime story'.

MARIE BASTING

'A delightfully engaging mystery, with a wonderful setting in 1930s Blackpool.'

KATHERINE WOODFINE

'A mystery with a gutsy new hero set against the fascinating backdrop of 1935 Blackpool Illuminations Switch-on. Rip-roaring action with conjurors, conmen and a secret society. If you like Robin Steven's *Murder Most Unladylike*, make way for Gracie Fairshaw.'

SARA GRANT

'Satisfyingly sprinkled with clues to sniff out, this is a timeless, accessible and well-paced mystery with bags of atmosphere.'

BOOKTRUST

'This heartwarming and gripping northern mystery is a summer must-read for both children and adults.'

STOOMIO

'I would thoroughly recommend this to both boys and girls of 8–12 years who enjoy an exciting, satisfying mystery story where the children are the real heroes.'

TOPPSTA (Reader review)

Also available by Susan Brownrigg

Gracie Fairshaw and the Mysterious Guest

Kintana and the Captain's Curse

Gracie Fairshaw and the Trouble at the Tower

Susan Brownrigg

uclanpublishing

Gracie Fairshaw and the Trouble at the Tower is a uclanpublishing book

First published in Great Britain in 2021 by
uclanpublishing
University of Central Lancashire
Preston, PR1 2HE, UK

978-1-9129-7959-2

3 5 7 9 10 8 6 4 2 1

Set in 10/17pt Kingfisher.

A CIP catalogue record for this book is available from the British Library.

Printed and bound in Great Britain by Clays Ltd, Elcograf S.p.A.

For Monica

Gracie Fairshaw and the Trouble at the Tower

Chapter One

The Dress Rehearsal

Wednesday 18th December, 1935

Gracie Fairshaw rubbed a large circle on the steamed-up window of the tram as it rattled along the prom. Wintry fog blended sand and sea into a wash of grey. She could barely see Blackpool Tower, but she knew they must be close.

The tram bell dinged twice. 'This is our stop!' cried her younger brother, George.

Gracie smoothed her bobble hat, making sure it covered her ears. Once the tram had halted, she followed George and the other passengers down to the lower deck, taking her time on the winding stairs.

As she stepped on to the promenade, the cold, salty air made her gasp after the warmth of the tram.

She paused for a moment while George tugged a cap over his scruffy blond hair, then she craned her neck to look up at the red brick Tower building. Huge letters across the front announcing, WONDERLAND OF THE WORLD. *It was true,* she thought, gazing at the posters and banners advertising the many attractions inside. No other town could boast of a building with an aquarium, circus, ballroom, menagerie, roof gardens *and* a 518-foot high cast iron tower!

Gracie and George grinned at each other excitedly. She gripped her brother's hand, waited for their tram to move on, then dashed across the tramlines and the road beyond to the Tower entrance.

'We're here for the Children's Ballet dress rehearsal,' she explained to the smartly dressed concierge at the door, passing him a letter of invitation. He checked it over and gave a nod. They sprinted up the grand staircase.

'We're to meet Violet and Tom by the Christmas tree,' said Gracie as she pushed open the doors to the ballroom.

'Wowsers! Look at all those presents!' cried George, running towards the gigantic fir tree in the centre of the dance floor.

Gracie hurried after him.

The Christmas tree was decorated in white, red and green

fairy lights and hundreds of gifts had been carefully balanced on its branches.

Violet and Tom waved as they got closer. It always tickled Gracie how alike they looked, although there was a year between the siblings. Violet at 14, was a bit older and taller than her brother, but they had the same dark red hair and freckles. Violet was wearing her favourite – now paint-splattered – dungarees and a checked shirt. Tom wore a pristine white shirt with matching blue blazer and trousers; everything perfectly ironed. They might look like peas in a pod, but their personalities were very different.

'Glad you could make it,' said Violet, hugging Gracie.

'The Christmas show is always amazing – and, best of all, we're seeing it for free,' said Tom. 'You're in for a real treat!'

'Thanks for inviting us,' said Gracie. 'I can't wait to see the sets you helped make, Violet.'

'It's just a few backdrops,' she replied, blushing.

George was still gawping at the tree. 'Who are all the presents for?'

'They'll be given out by Father Christmas to members of the League of the Shining Star at a special Christmas Eve party,' replied Tom.

'Ooh, that means we can go this year,' said George, eyeing up one of the biggest presents.

'Yes, but remember Ma said Father Christmas only gives

gifts to well-behaved children,' teased Gracie.

'I'm a little angel,' replied George, his eyes twinkling mischievously.

Gracie and her friends laughed.

Violet hooked her arm around Gracie's left arm, which ended just past her elbow. 'Isn't the tree amazing,' she said.

Gracie nodded. 'It's beautiful.'

'Beautiful? Oh, yes, I suppose it is, only I meant the size of it. *The Gazette* says it's fifty-foot high! Mr Chadwick, the caretaker, says they had to cut it in half to get it into the ballroom. Imagine the size of the saw they must've used!'

Gracie grinned. 'Most lasses would be excited about the decorations on the tree, not the lumber skills needed to install it.'

'*Pah*, to most lasses,' replied Violet.

'Remember the last time we were in here?' asked Tom, as they all made their way over to a row of red velvet seats facing the stage.

'I don't think I'll ever forget,' replied Gracie, with a shudder. She and George had befriended Tom and Violet Emberton after Ma disappeared suddenly from the Fairshaw's new boarding house that September. They had helped investigate which of The Majestic guests were responsible and then rescued her.

'I think the Tower Ballroom is my favourite place in Blackpool,' said Tom, as they settled into their seats.

'It is very special. It's like being inside a palace, not that

I've ever been in one!' Gracie beamed as she looked round at the golden balconies, glass skylight, painted ceiling murals and twinkling crystal chandeliers. It was magical.

A tall woman with a stern expression, her black hair pulled back into a tight bun, entered the ballroom from the staff-only door beside the stage. She was dressed all in black with a woollen shawl wrapped around her slender body. She used a cane, as she made her way to a seat directly facing the centre of the stage. She was escorted by a thin man who wore round spectacles and a battered brown suit.

'That's Madame Petrova, the ballet director,' whispered Tom. 'She hasn't been in charge very long.'

There was a man sitting at the piano, in front of the stage, Gracie noticed he looked rather flustered as he flicked through his sheet music.

The stage curtains opened revealing a festive setting. There was a toy box, a lovely rocking horse and Father Christmas's golden sleigh filled with wrapped parcels.

'The backdrops look marvellous, Violet,' whispered Gracie. 'You are clever for making them.'

Violet shrugged. 'The fake windows were pretty straight-forward – that toy box was trickier, I spent ages getting those hinges right. Still, Mr Chadwick was pleased in the end. Did I tell you the first lot were accidentally thrown away?'

'Yes, you did,' replied Gracie. 'Lucky for you though.'

'Mr Chadwick was in a right panic!' Violet continued, rolling her eyes. 'He was a bit reluctant to hire a girl, but I was the first to apply for the job and he had a tight deadline to meet. That's one advantage of Pa working for *The Gazette*, I get a sneak preview of any job opportunities! I'm hoping Mr Chadwick will offer me more work now. I could learn loads working alongside him.'

'I need to find a job, now I've left school an' all,' replied Gracie. 'We won't have many guests staying at The Majestic between Christmas and Easter. I don't want Ma to cut Phyllis's hours. If I can earn some wages, it would make a big difference. I don't suppose you've heard of any openings at the Tower?'

Violet shook her head. 'I'll let you know if I do. The problem is, there'll be lots of people in the same situation as you. Most jobs in Blackpool are seasonal. I'll let you know if I see anything in *The Gazette* though.'

***

Three ballet dancers walked on to the stage. The youngest was petite with blonde hair and striking blue eyes. Gracie thought she looked a couple of year's younger than herself, maybe around twelve. The other two girls were older, maybe fifteen or sixteen, the shorter girl had raven black hair and pale skin, the other girl looked an outdoorsy type; she was statuesque with brown hair and green eyes. They were all

identically dressed in white leotards and tutus, their hair pulled back in a bun.

Another girl hurried on to the stage, brushing a loose strand of hair from her face.

'Gosh,' said Gracie, 'isn't that Audrey Mosson?'

The gang had befriended Audrey during their search for Ma.

'It is an' all!' said Violet.

'I knew she loved to dance, but I didn't realise she'd gone professional,' said Tom, impressed.

'Audrey!' called George.

'Don't,' hushed Violet. 'The Children's Ballet dancers have to follow a series of strict rules of behaviour. Top of the list is a ban on speaking to Tower staff or visitors.'

'Music,' ordered Madame, pointing her cane.

The pianist began to play a Christmassy tune.

The raven-haired girl completed a series of fast turns, her golden tutu glinted under the spotlights as she leapt forward in a perfect *grand jeté*, feet pointed, fingers stretched out.

'You can see why Natalya is the ballerina,' said Tom.

'Aren't they all ballerinas?' asked Gracie, confused.

'That's a common mistake to make. The other girls are *ballet dancers*,' explained Tom. 'Ballerina is a special title; it is given to the principal dancer. "Natalya is Madame's daughter, but she's clearly been given the role because of her grace and passion for dance.'

Gracie and Tom were enthralled by the girls' skill – George and Violet less so, but at least Violet was a bit more discreet about it. George passed the time by picking his nose and examining the results.

At last, it was Audrey's moment in the spotlight. Gracie smiled as her friend moved gracefully towards the centre of the stage, her arms raised as she began to pirouette.

She circled round and round the stage, but when the dancer reached stage right, Gracie noticed the scenery begin to topple. She jumped up.

'Look out!' she yelled.

It was too late, the scenery fell, knocking Audrey forward.

'*Ow!*' she cried, as she smacked on to the floor.

Gracie gasped.

'Oh no!' gasped Violet.

Gracie felt a cold sensation plunge to the pit of her stomach as she ran up the stage steps after Violet. Tom, George, the pianist and Madame Petrova at their heels. She hoped Audrey hadn't been badly hurt.

She tried to see past the other dancers. The girls looked strange up close; their faces heavy with white powder and painted-in features. There was something menacing about their make-up, like a mask.

'Out of the way, girls,' ordered Madame Petrova.

Gracie had already bent down to lift the scenery off Audrey's leg. Violet, Tom and George each grabbed a corner. Luckily, it wasn't heavy, only a bit awkward to lift.

Audrey moaned as the wood shifted. She slid her leg out, and they lowered the scenery to one side.

The pianist was calming the youngest girl, who was crying loudly.

'Ruth, compose yourself.' Madame Petrova pointed her cane at the man. 'Don't fuss over her, Mr Linnet. Fetch one of those seats up for Audrey.'

'Of course, Madame,' the pianist replied, adjusting his glasses and dashing down the steps.

'Will she be all right, Madame Petrova?' asked the young blonde dancer, a sob in her throat.

'If you give me some space, I will be able to find out, Ruth.' The ballet director spoke with a strong Russian accent as she brushed the girl away. 'Audrey, do you think you can stand?'

She moaned. 'It hurts, but I think so.'

The older girls looked anxiously at her and helped her up. Audrey leant into the tallest girl as she tried to put weight on her ankle.

Mr Linnet had returned with one of the red velvet chairs.

'Sit down so I can take a closer look,' said Madame Petrova.

'Bet it's broken,' said George.

'Shush,' said Gracie. 'Hopefully it's only a sprain.'

Madame Petrova crouched down, 'I suspect you have

damaged the muscle.' She carefully felt along Audrey's ankle, causing the dancer to grimace. The director stood up. 'Yes, as I suspected. No permanent damage, but you must rest it for at least one week.'

'Oh no,' cried Audrey. 'The show's run will be over by then.'

The other girls gasped.

'What a disaster,' said the girl with brown hair. 'The whole show will have to be rewritten.'

'It cannot be helped, Frances,' said Madame Petrova, with a slight shrug.

'But Madame, Audrey is *first soloist*,' said Ruth.

'One of you will have to replace her.'

The girls all looked at Frances. *They must think Madame Petrova will choose her*, thought Gracie.

The director clapped her hands. Her grey eyes were steely with determination. 'The show will go on. We continue to rehearse.'

'But, Madame, what if this wasn't an accident? What if someone deliberately pushed the scenery over?' asked Ruth, her cheeks pinking.

Gracie knitted her brow. *Why would she be worried about that? It didn't seem very likely.*

'Don't be silly,' replied Madame Petrova. 'This is no one's fault.'

'I have to disagree,' said Mr Linnet, firmly. 'Ruth has a valid point. That scenery should not have toppled. It must have been badly constructed. I hate to say it, but I'm afraid Mr Chadwick may be to blame.'

Violet paled. Her voice trembled as she spoke, 'But Mr Chadwick isn't responsible. I am!'

Chapter Two

Itching for Success

Madame Petrova waggled her cane. 'And who are you? Stand up straight, child.'

'I'm Violet Emberton,' Violet replied, her voice shaking under the ballet director's glare. 'I worked on that backdrop, not Mr Chadwick.'

'You could have killed Audrey!' cried Ruth.

'Don't exaggerate,' said Madame. 'It's not solid oak.'

'I don't understand why it fell,' said Violet, confused.

'I'm sure it was just an accident,' Gracie reassured her.

'*Are you*?' questioned Frances. 'Didn't Natalya warn us summat bad was going to happen?'

'Girls!' scolded Madame Petrova.

'And I was right. I don't think they were aiming for you,

Audrey,' continued Natalya, her hands curling into fists. 'I think they meant to hurt me.'

Ruth gasped. 'You think the let–'

Madame rapped her cane. 'Enough of this nonsense.' She gave a little shake of her head, recomposing herself. 'Mr Linnet, please fetch Mr Chadwick from backstage. I want this scenery made safe. No more delays.'

Mr Linnet nodded. 'Of course, Madame.'

'I didn't know Audrey was first soloist,' whispered Tom, 'Madame must think she's good enough to become a ballerina! She'll be so disappointed if this injury interrupts her career.'

'The rest of you, get changed for the next scene,' said Madame. 'Ruth, I have decided you will take Audrey's place in the show.'

'Me?' She sounded terrified. 'I mean, thank you, Madame.'

Frances's face was wide open like a codfish. She closed it slowly. 'Congratulations, Ruth.'

'Yes, well done,' said Audrey.

'Yes, congratulations,' added Natalya, quietly.

'That's enough fuss,' said Madame Petrova. 'Ruth, take Audrey to Natalya's dressing room. She won't manage the stairs with that ankle. Frances, ask the concierge to call Audrey's father. Explain she has had a fall and that he needs to collect her.'

'Yes, Madame.'

The ballet director ushered Audrey, Ruth and Natalya backstage. At the last moment, the ballerina turned and glared at Violet. Madame Petrova might not blame her friend for the accident, but her daughter clearly did.

* * *

Gracie had to find proof that Violet was not responsible for the accident. 'Come on,' she said, once they were alone in the ballroom. 'I want to examine that scenery.'

They grouped around the fake window. Gracie kneeled. 'The stabilising foot has come loose.' That didn't seem quite right to Gracie – she knew her friend was diligent; she would have made sure everything was perfect.

'So that's why it fell over,' said Tom.

'It was fine when I attached it. I'm certain,' insisted Violet.

'We believe you,' said Tom. 'This isn't your fault.'

'The dancers think it is,' said George. 'They looked like they wanted to slap you!'

'George!' scolded Tom. 'It was an accident.'

'I'm afraid not,' said Gracie, wiggling the foot. 'Someone has deliberately taken some of the screws out. No wonder it toppled over.' *Ruth's fears seem to be right,* she thought.

'But who would do that?' asked Tom, aghast. 'Who would want to harm Audrey?'

'Whoever did it, couldn't be sure when it would fall, could they?' pondered Gracie aloud.

'Maybe they didn't care who it squashed,' said George.

'How horrid,' said Gracie, 'but I think you might be right.'

'What a nasty thing to do,' tutted Violet.

'Now, now, out of my way,' called Neville Chadwick, appearing from backstage with Mr Linnet. The caretaker looked hot and bothered; sweat on his brow.

'The foot needs tightening,' called Violet, as the men came nearer. 'I can give you a hand if you like.'

'I think you've caused enough bother,' said Mr Chadwick. 'I should never have hired a girl. They're going to blame me for taking you on, just liked they blamed me for the first lot of scenery being thrown away by mistake.'

'I just hope the rest of the scenery isn't dangerous, Neville,' added Mr Linnet. 'Skedaddle, you kids.'

The gang scurried down the stage steps.

'Should we go?' asked Violet, her face was flushed with embarrassment.

'No,' whispered Gracie. 'I've got a bad feeling. First, the scenery gets dumped and then the new backdrop falls on Audrey. What if someone is trying to get Mr Chadwick sacked?'

'It's not me,' said Violet, eyes wide.

'Of course not,' said Tom. 'But maybe Gracie's right. Perhaps we should stick around.'

* * *

Ten minutes later, Madame Petrova led the dancers back on

to the stage. Frances and Ruth had changed into grey leotards, tights and silver waistcoats with pretend turn keys attached to the back. Top hats with a coloured feather completed their transformation into tin soldiers.

'Don't they look fabulous,' whispered Tom.

Gracie smiled and nodded, but her mind was on Violet. What if Mr Chadwick started telling other people her friend was to blame for the accident.

Natalya, the ballerina, was dressed differently to the other two. She wore a red striped top, red shorts with braces and a matching felt cap. Two red circles of rouge had been applied to her cheeks.

Mr Linnet was at the piano again. He pushed his glasses back up his nose and rummaged in a battered leather case designed for carrying sheet music. He pulled out a wad of paper and offered it to the ballet director, but she wafted it away with disinterest.

'Not now, Mr Linnet. Make yourself useful, please, and assist Natalya, we cannot afford to waste more time,' she ordered, bending over to massage her knee.

The pianist mumbled under his breath, then climbed the stage steps and disappeared into the wing. Something was being lowered from above the stage.

Gracie narrowed her eyes – it was a harness with a set of puppet strings attached, complete with crossbar.

Mr Linnet helped Natalya into the harness. The ballerina seemed strangely nervous. She wriggled as he tested it was secure.

'Keep still,' snapped Madame Petrova.

Gracie was distracted by a movement in the shadows. Someone was watching the performance from the left wing. An old woman with untidy white hair. She looked like she was about to step out on to the stage.

Gracie nudged Tom to look, just as someone pulled the woman back into the stage wing.

'Well I never,' whispered Tom. 'I'm sure that was Mrs Waters! She was ballet director before Madame Petrova. She oversaw the Blackpool Tower Children's Ballet for donkey's years. She and "Little Miri" retired earlier this year.'

'Who is Little Miri?' asked Gracie.

'She is Blackpool's most famous child star,' Tom explained. 'She was only five when she joined the ballet. Mrs Waters doted on her – in fact, she went on to adopt her.'

'Will she be in the show?'

'Oh no, Miriam is all grown up,' Tom explained. 'I'm surprised at Mrs Waters creeping around backstage though. Do you think she's spying on her predecessor?'

'Perhaps she's come to wish the girls well,' said Gracie, with a shrug.

The pianist secured the final grip, then dashed back to

his instrument and began to play. It was a jaunty tune with a rhythm like a ticking clock.

Natalya threw out her arms in a jerky manner then kicked out her legs; left, right, left, right.

'Very modern,' said Tom.

The ballerina tossed her head sharply to one side, then the other. She really was like a puppet brought to life!

Natalya had such complete control over every step – every move in perfect timing with the music.

But then something changed, a pained look spread across Natalya's face. She seemed to miss a beat, her shoulders rolling in discomfort.

Another misstep. Natalya seemed to jolt before stumbling forward.

Madame Petrova banged her cane on the floor. 'No, no, what are you doing?' she barked.

Something was wrong.

Natalya twitched and flinched awkwardly. Her shoulders jerked, her arms shot into the air and she flapped her hands around her head. Then she lurched from side to side, with a groan and shudder. Her face turning the colour of beetroot.

The other dancers had come to a stop and were pointing at Natalya.

Gracie cringed, feeling the girl's embarrassment.

All attempts at dance had been lost. Natalya's hands were

all over her body, her fingers scratching at her skin. She pulled off her harness.

'What are you doing?' cried Madame Petrova.

Natalya tugged at her striped top. 'Oh, oh! It itches, it itches!' Her skin was turning as red as her make-up. A blotchy rash spread over her arms and neck.

George giggled. 'Someone's put itching powder in her pants!'

'It's not funny,' said Gracie. 'It must really hurt.'

'Natalya, go and wash it off,' ordered Madame Petrova, as the ballerina ran off stage. 'And Frances, Ruth – you are dismissed too.'

The pair looked at each other, their brows wrinkled with confusion.

'Dismissed . . .' Ruth hesitated. 'Do you mean practice is *cancelled*?'

The director lifted her head. 'Yes. Go! Get out! I cannot concentrate with all this nonsense. Be warned, if there is *one* more incident,' she wagged her finger. 'One more mishap and I will cancel the whole show. Madame Petrova does not work with *amateurs*.'

'This isn't the girls' fault,' argued Mr Linnet. 'I don't know why you're shouting at them.'

But Madame was in no mood for listening. She stormed off the stage and across the ballroom floor.

Mr Linnet sighed and gathered up his music, muttering under his breath, before he too exited the room.

'Madame Petrova won't really cancel *Winter Belles*, will she?' asked Violet.

'She can't!' said Tom. 'It's a Blackpool tradition! Think of all the families looking forward to seeing the show.'

'Gracie, you've got to find out what's going on,' said George. 'You are great at solving mysteries!'

'We can help again,' said Violet. 'We already have some puzzle pieces!'

'If someone is deliberately targeting the Children's Ballet, we should try and find out who and why!' said Gracie.

'We can ask Audrey what she knows,' said Tom. 'We should go and check on her, any road.'

Violet stared at the floor. 'What if she doesn't want to see me.'

'Don't be silly. Besides, you're the only one who knows their way around backstage,' said Gracie.

* * *

Natalya's dressing room was surprisingly plain. There was a dressing table with a large mirror, two battered chairs, a chest, a large wardrobe and a dressmaker's dummy covered with a long Father Christmas-style cape with a fur-trimmed hood. The wallpaper was peeling behind a series of faded posters advertising past shows.

Audrey was sitting on one of the chairs with her foot elevated on another.

'How is your ankle?' asked Gracie. 'Is it very sore?'

'A little, but I'll be fine. I just need to rest it for a few days. My dad is coming to collect me.'

Gracie told Audrey all about the itching powder.

'What an awful trick to play. I can't believe one of the girls would do that. They're all lovely.'

'Sometimes people *pretend* to be nice when inside they're rotten with jealousy.'

'Violet's right,' agreed Gracie, 'it could be anyone here at the Tower, including the other dancers. We saw Mrs Waters backstage, she's the first of our suspects, but there may be more.'

'Mrs Waters? She wouldn't do anything malicious against the Tower Ballet, she loves it,' said Audrey. 'But if you want a list of people to question, you should keep this.' She picked up a blue and gold programme from the dressing table.

Gracie opened the booklet. Inside there were advertisements for refreshments – ginger ales and sparkling fruit sodas, chocolates and pastilles – as well as promotions for the Tower Circus and Ballroom.

In the centre was a double-page spread with a photograph of the ballet dancers.

Gracie recognised Audrey, Natalya and the other two girls. She pointed at the young blonde. 'That's Ruth, isn't it?'

'That's right, she's a nice quiet girl,' said Audrey, 'Frances is the older, taller girl. I'm rather surprised Madame Petrova didn't choose her to take over my role. Frances is very protective of the younger dancers, quite the mother hen, perhaps it's because she has no family of her own, but her bark's worse than her bite.'

Gracie thought Audrey had summed up the girls rather well.

'Blimey,' said George, reading over her shoulder. 'It says summat about a ballet corpse! If I'd known there was going to be dead bodies in the show, I'd have paid more attention.'

'*Corps de ballet*,' corrected Tom. 'They're a bit like the chorus. Natalya is the ballerina, then there are the soloists – the girls we saw today – and then up to a hundred other performers that make up the "body" of the ballet.'

'Oh,' said George, disappointed. 'You're sure it doesn't mean there are zombies in it?'

'Sorry, pal.'

Gracie shook her head and continued to read the programme while the others chatted.

Madame Petrova was listed as the show's director and producer. The arranger was Harry Linnet, the pianist; Fredini and his dance band would provide the music. The only person not mentioned was Neville Chadwick.

'Oh, Ruth Linnet – that's the same as the pianist,' said Gracie.

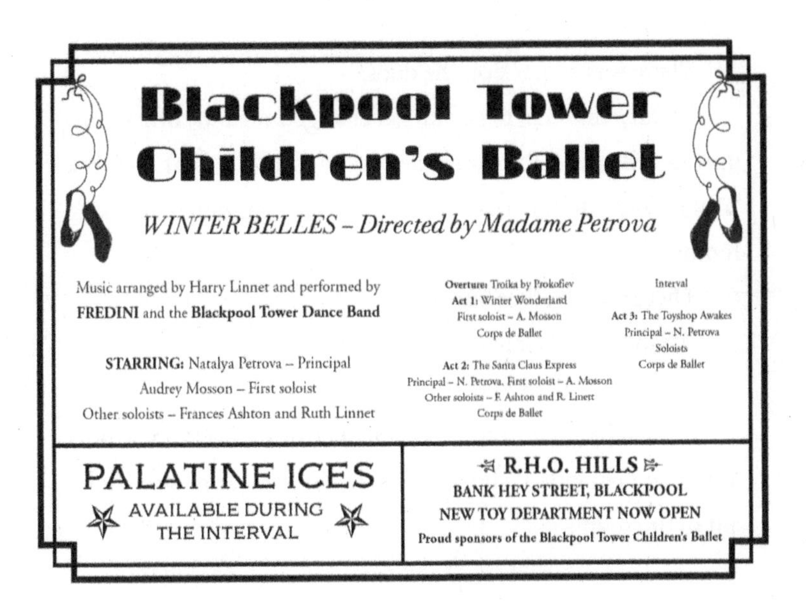

'Ruth's his daughter,' said Audrey. 'Mr Linnet played for Mrs Waters for years. It made sense for Ruth to start ballet lessons.'

'That's really useful, thanks Audrey,' Gracie replied. 'It's a shame you're out of action, it would be useful to have a dancer who could spy for us. . .'

'Don't ask Violet to audition,' teased Tom. 'She's more chance of joining the elephant troop the way she stomps about.'

'Well, they definitely won't let you in,' snapped Violet. 'It's girls only, remember.'

'Thank goodness,' said George.

'Dancing's not my strong point either,' said Gracie.

There was a knock on the door.

'Natalya has had to go and get changed with the other girls, upstairs, because I'm using her room,' Audrey said, quickly. 'You'll find all the costumes near the communal dressing rooms.'

There was another knock.

'Thanks,' said Gracie.

'Come in,' called Audrey.

It was her dad and Madame Petrova. 'Everybody out,' Madame demanded, shooing Gracie, George, Tom and Violet out of the room.

* * *

'Madame Petrova's scary, isn't she?' commented Violet, as they made their way back to the foyer.

'She looks like a vulture.'

'George!' Gracie spluttered.

'She does a bit,' said Violet with a grin. 'It's that black feathery shawl and the way she hunches over.

'She seems quite strict, but I suppose you need to be disciplined to be a ballet director,' said Gracie. 'I think she has a lot of pain with her knee, probably her back too.'

'Ballet dancers can really suffer with injuries and it's not a long-term job, that's why they often move into teaching,' said Tom. 'Madame Petrova was one of Russia's most renowned ballerinas.'

Gracie only half-listened, her mind ticking over. 'We should inspect the costumes. George, have you got your magnifying glass with you?'

'Of course. Detectives always carry a magnifying glass!' He reached into his coat pocket and thrust it at Gracie.

Gracie led the others back out into the corridor. A signpost marked DRESSING ROOMS directed them upstairs.

They climbed three flights of narrow stairs, the sound of the dancers' chatter getting steadily louder.

Gracie followed the noise along a corridor. The way was partially blocked by two clothes rails on wheels.

Gracie and Violet examined them while Tom guarded the stairs and George kept an eye on the other end of the corridor. The first was filled with discarded costumes for cleaning, pressing or repairs. Gracie recognised Natayla's red puppet costume and the girls' tin soldier outfits. The second rail held soft, feathery skirts and long white cotton nightdresses.

Each costume was labelled with the girl's name. Gracie and Violet inspected the unused costumes first, but they were all perfectly ordinary. They moved on to Natalya's clothing. 'Look!' said Gracie, adjusting the magnifying glass over the red shorts so Violet could see. 'The itching powder is actually tiny little hairs! It's on her striped top too.'

Gracie opened her shoulder bag and took out a compact mirror. 'We need to collect the evidence,' she said. 'We could do

with something to brush the hairs on to the mirror . . .'

'I've got a pair of tweezers in my satchel,' Violet offered.

Gracie raised an eyebrow. 'Since when did you start using tweezers?'

'They're for splinters,' said Violet.

'I should have known!'

Violet rummaged in her bag for them.

They worked as a team. Violet carefully removed several thin strands using the tweezers, while Gracie held the open compact.

'Excellent.' Gracie snapped it shut, just as the sound of some kind of kerfuffle came from the far end of the corridor.

'Let me past!' demanded a voice. It was Natalya.

'Stop!' shouted George, but the ballerina was thundering towards Gracie and Violet. He chased after her.

Chapter Three

A Poisoned Pen

'What are you doing to our costumes?' demanded Natalya. She was dressed in a bath robe, her skin still pink.

'Girls! Help!' she called out.

Frances and Ruth came running out of their communal dressing room and down the corridor. They looked like ordinary girls in their normal clothes, their faces wiped clean and their hair down.

'You're not allowed up here,' said Frances, hands on hips.

'They were doing something to the costumes,' said Natalya, checking through the clothes rail herself. 'I reckon they were going to steal one.'

'That's not true. We were just looking at your puppet outfit,' said Gracie.

'We found itching powder all over it,' added Violet.

'You put it there, you mean, and now you're trying to hide the proof,' said Frances. She pointed at Violet. 'And you made the scenery fall on Audrey.'

The girls gathered in a line. They were very intimidating.

Luckily, the shouting had alerted Tom too. So they were now four versus three. Gracie felt relieved.

'Audrey's our friend! I wouldn't hurt her on purpose,' argued Violet.

'You might have done it out of jealousy,' said Natalya.

'There are hundreds of girls who want to join the Tower Ballet every year,' added Frances proudly.

'Don't be a numbskull,' said Violet. 'I don't want to be a dancer.'

'Yeah,' agreed George. 'She doesn't want to flap around on stage like an upside-down flamingo.'

Frances's mouth fell open. 'You cheeky monkey!'

'George! Apologise,' scolded Gracie.

'It's Frances that should apologise,' said Ruth. 'What would Auntie Astra say if she heard you saying such awful things?'

Tom and Violet smiled knowingly at each other. Auntie Astra wrote the League of the Shining Star a children's page for the Gazette. What the girls didn't realise, was that it was actually written by their pa, Blackpool's publicity officer.

Frances opened and closed her hand like a shining star, to show she was a member of the paper's children's club. Ruth copied her, then prompted Natalya to do the same.

'We're all in the Children's League of the Shining Star too,' said Gracie, as they all returned the signal. 'You know, as club members, we have to help each other. It's what we swore to do when we joined.'

The girls looked to each other. They seemed torn. The silence seemed to go on for ever.

'Listen, girls,' said Ruth finally, nervously twisting her blonde hair. 'We've tried to find out who is causing trouble at the Tower, and we've failed. Now with these new attacks, I think Gracie's right, we need help.'

'If we put our heads together, I reckon we can work out who is responsible,' said Gracie.

'We do not have any better ideas, do we?' said Natalya.

'Let's go into the practice room,' added Frances, 'so we can be sure no one will overhear.'

They all walked down the corridor into a room with two rows of back-to-back wooden benches with metal pegs above. Names and initials had been scratched into the wood. There was room for about eight girls to get changed at once. Gracie shuddered at the thought of the room crammed full of dancers bickering over who got what space and squabbling over costumes.

Natalya and the others beckoned them to a spot at the far end which looked like it was used for ballet practice. There was a series of full-length mirrors with a long wooden barre for dancers to use when running through their warm-up exercises.

Gracie could see her reflection next to the other girls and she stood straighter, conscious of their perfect posture.

'You must see this,' said Natalya. She reached into her dressing gown pocket, pulled out a pale blue envelope and passed it over. 'It arrived with some fan mail.'

'It's a poison pen letter,' said Ruth, grimacing.

Frances hugged her.

'How horrid!' Gracie studied the envelope first. PETROVA was written in letters so straight that she suspected a stencil or ruler had been used to form each one.

Three fingerprints in white paint were on the edge. *That was clumsy of them*, Gracie thought.

There was no stamp on the envelope. She turned it over. No return address on the back, just an embossed trademark. She studied it closer, it was a jowly dog. The paper was manufactured by the British Bulldog paper company.

Gracie placed the envelope into the crook of her left elbow and eased out the contents. She unfolded the matching pale blue paper.

The message had been spelt out in letters from newspaper headlines. Each one carefully cut out and then pasted down.

YOU ARE NOT WANTED HERE LEAVE OR YOU WILL REGRET IT

'What a nasty, bitter thing to write,' said Gracie, passing the letter on for Tom, Violet and George to see. 'And you have no idea who might have sent it?'

Natalya shook her head.

'Have you showed it to your mother?' asked Tom.

She shook her head again. 'Mama has enough to worry about with the show. We thought we could find the – culprit, is that the word? – ourselves.'

'I think we can assume whoever wrote this letter also made the scenery fall. That could explain the fingerprints on the envelope – and I bet they put the itching powder in your costume too. Have there been any other incidents or accidents?' Gracie asked.

Ruth's face flushed. 'Someone scribbled all over my pa's sheet music.'

'That's nasty,' said Violet.

'It could have been one of the "babies",' said Frances.

'Babies?' asked George. 'They can't dance.'

'It's what we call the youngest girls,' Frances explained.

Ruth smiled at her. 'Poor pa, he's having a tough time, He was hoping Mrs Waters would introduce him to her song sheet publishers. She and Little Miri have had a few big hits, but Madame Petrova doesn't have the same contacts. If he could get someone interested in his compositions, he could make a lot of money.'

'I see.' Gracie took the letter back from George and passed it to Natalya. She couldn't help wondering if Mr Linnet was more frustrated than his daughter realised. Could he have scribbled on his own music in anger and then decided to sabotage Madame's ballet? 'Anything else?'

'My Father Christmas cape was stolen,' said Natalya. 'And all our ballet shoes keep disappearing. Mama thinks I am making an elephant out of a fly. That these are only childish pranks, like when we found salt in our sugar bowl.'

'But that scenery falling over wasn't a silly joke,' said Frances.

Gracie thought back to the accident. There had been someone else backstage – could they have been responsible for the scenery falling? She didn't want to make an outright accusation and rile the girls further, so she said, in as casual a voice as she could manage, 'We saw Mrs Waters off stage.

I suppose she came to wish you all well?'

Ruth and Frances exchanged glances, 'Mrs Waters? You must be mistaken,' said the blonde.

'It will have been Mr Chadwick or one of the technicians,' agreed Frances.

'It was definitely Mrs Waters,' said Tom, backing up Gracie.

'Was Mrs Waters upset at being replaced?' asked Violet. 'Could her nose be put out that someone younger has taken control of the ballet?'

'Her *nose*?' repeated Natalya.

'It's an expression,' Ruth explained.

'You think the ex-ballet director did this?' asked Natalya.

'You're mistaken. Mrs Waters is lovely,' said Frances. 'She has taught us all ballet since we were tots.'

'She wouldn't want to hurt any of us,' agreed Ruth, twisting her hair again.

'Didn't you both say she's been acting strangely, lately?' asked Natalya. 'And why does she keep "popping in",' she continued. 'Mama was really fed up with her surprise visits even *before* she nearly caused a flood. The cleaners had to mop up the toilets for hours after Mrs Waters left the taps running.'

'That was just an accident,' said Frances.

Gracie's ears pricked. What if it hadn't been an accident? What if Mrs Waters had done it on purpose?

'Mrs Waters was happy to retire,' continued Frances. 'She

understood the Children's Ballet needs a younger director, someone with modern ideas.'

'Well, Madame Petrova definitely fits the bill,' said Tom.

Natalya looked confused again.

'It means she is perfect for the job,' said Ruth.

'Does anyone not like your mama?' asked Gracie.

The girls looked at each other.

'Only the caretaker,' muttered Frances. Ruth jabbed her.

'Mr Chadwick?' asked Violet.

'Frances thinks he has a soft spot for Mrs Waters,' said Ruth.

'A soft spot? He's absolutely smitten. I bet there's a shrine to her in his workshop!'

'Don't be silly, Frances,' said Ruth. 'Sometimes you talk such rubbish.'

'I was only joking.'

'Perhaps we should go to the police with the letter,' said Natalya, her face anguished. 'In case they strike again?'

'They won't take us seriously,' said Ruth. 'No one takes children seriously.'

'Not without proper proof,' said Frances.

'Well, we'll get some,' said George, 'Won't we, Gracie?'

'We can try,' she replied. 'I need to think of a way that I can question the adults about what they might have seen.'

They left the girls to get changed and made their way

downstairs and back through the ballroom. 'We have our first suspects,' said George, gleefully. 'But how do we know which one is the baddie?'

Chapter Four

Monkey Business

The gang decided to talk through what they had learnt so far over hot chocolates. The best place for those, they agreed, was the Tower's Oriental Lounge.

Gracie looked up in awe at the Tower's legs that arched over her head like a golden rainbow as they entered the Chinese-themed cafe. The Oriental Lounge was one of her favourite parts of the Tower because of its deep red colour and pagoda style decoration, complete with dragons and masks. It was like being in a different country!

The lounge was a popular place to get refreshments when the queues were long for the Tower Ascent lifts. In the middle of December though, there were plenty of free tables.

Gracie, George, Tom and Violet chose one in a corner away

from any other visitors.

'It's ages till teatime. I'm starving. Can we get an ice cream too?' asked George.

'In *this* weather?' Gracie raised her eyebrows. 'It's freezing out!'

'Well, the monkeys are having one,' he replied, pointing to a table next to a large potted palm. Two chimpanzees in frilly dresses were sitting, sharing a bowl of ice cream, overseen by a frazzled looking zoo keeper. He wore a green uniform with matching peaked cap.

Gracie giggled. 'You wouldn't see that in Milltown!' The chimp in pink was licking the bowl clean. She'd seen George do the same many a time.

A young waitress in a 1920's Shanghai-style dress approached the table. Her name tag said *Lin Ng* and she seemed to be the only person taking orders. *No wonder she looked frazzled,* thought Gracie, noting the shadows under her eyes.

'What would you like?' asked Lin, in a thick Liverpudlian accent.

Tom and Violet were still reading the menu.

'Two hot chocolates please, Lin,' said Gracie.

'And a banana split,' added George.

'Go on then.' Gracie nodded her approval. 'And I'll have a warm mince pie with cream. Thank you.'

'We'll have the same as you, Gracie,' replied Violet after conferring with Tom.

'Do you want cream on your hot chocolate?'

They all nodded.

Lin jotted down their order and then hurried back to the kitchen.

'I've been wondering about Mrs Waters,' said Violet. 'If she just wanted to see the dress rehearsal, surely she wouldn't be hiding in the shadows. What if she's jealous of a younger woman taking over her job?'

'We need to find out if Mrs Waters really *was* happy to leave the ballet,' agreed Tom.

'Then there's Mr Chadwick, the caretaker,' Gracie continued. 'He also has access backstage. Frances reckons he has romantic feelings for Mrs Waters. What if he's trying to get rid of Madame Petrova so that Mrs Waters can get her job back?'

'But he's ever so nice,' said Violet. 'I don't think it can be him.'

'You only like him 'cause he gave you a job,' said George.

'Of course, there is another possibility,' said Gracie, placing a napkin on her lap. 'It could be that one of the dancers is jealous of Natalya and wants the role for herself. I think we can safely rule out Audrey, as she was hurt, and besides, we know she wouldn't do anything like that, but we don't know these other girls. It could be that Ruth or Frances wants the senior girls out of the ballet so they will get the best parts.'

The others murmured in agreement.

Lin had returned, carrying a tray. 'Here you are,' she said, trying to stifle a yawn.

They thanked her, as she passed out their orders.

George's banana split was served with a topping of nuts and chocolate sauce, while the mince pies were huge, with generous dollops of whipped cream.

They all sipped their hot chocolate, laughing at each other's cream moustaches.

The bowl was warm to the touch, as Gracie pulled it a little closer. She cut into the soft pastry with her spoon and mixed it with a little of the cream before tasting it. The sweet mincemeat and creaminess melted on her tongue. It was delicious. She chopped another chunk off and popped it into her mouth, letting the Christmassy flavour linger.

George, meanwhile, filled his mouth like a stoker shovelling coal into a steam train's firebox.

'Ooh, miss! Duck!' called the zoo keeper, as the chimp in yellow slung the plastic bowl across the room. It landed with a clatter next to Gracie's shoes.

George sniggered.

'Watch out,' said Tom.

The keeper was on his feet. 'Mandy, you little madam! Just because I said you couldn't have seconds.' The chimp seemed to be laughing, her teeth on show, as she bounced off her chair and raced after the bowl. 'Come back here!'

'They're not taking much notice,' said Violet.

Mandy turned and stuck her tongue out. Then she picked up the bowl and clanged it over and over on the floor.

'This is brilliant; better than the circus,' said George.

Lin was apologising to all the customers for the disruption. Gracie felt a pang of empathy.

The waitress ducked into the kitchen.

The chimp ran towards their table. Gracie leant down to Mandy and spoke softly. 'Go on. Return to your table.'

'Careful,' said Tom.

The ape stared, as though listening, then she gave a loud shriek and flipped the bowl on to Gracie's head.

'Oh, Gracie!' said Violet.

George howled with laughter. 'Oh no, the other chimp's coming now,' he stuttered between gasps for air. Tears streaming down his face.

Gracie lifted the bowl off and wiped away drips of ice cream with a napkin. George was right. The chimp in pink had clambered off her chair and scurried, knuckles against the ground, towards her pal.

Lin was back, armed with a mop and bucket. She tried to clean the mess made by the chimps.

'Leave that!' snapped the keeper, batting away the mop handle. He rubbed his hairy chin, then blew into a whistle which dangled on a string around his neck. 'Hilda! Get out here. Now!'

Suddenly, a girl about Gracie's age bolted out of the lavatories, fastening up her dungarees as she ran.

'I was as quick as I could be Mr Ramsbottom,' said Hilda, wiping her hands on the back of her uniform. 'I'd have wet myself if I waited any longer.'

The chimps were racing round and round, flinging their arms around and chattering to each other.

'They're going to have a job catching them,' said Violet.

Hilda rolled her eyes at the waitress. 'Lin! Why on earth did you give them ice cream?'

'Mr Ramsbottom insisted,' replied Lin, her voice trembling as she backed away.

'I was testing out a new idea for their tea party act,' said the zoo keeper. 'I thought sundaes would be funny.'

'Well, I'm not laughing,' said Hilda, under her breath. 'And neither is Lin. Look at this mess! She's going to be in even more trouble now.'

Poor Lin, thought Gracie, as the cook's raised voice bellowed out from the kitchen. 'Lin, this is your final warning!'

The zoo keeper smirked. 'It's her job to clean up after customers.'

'It's not Lin's job to clean up after animals, though, is it?' replied Hilda, between gritted teeth. 'How on earth are we going to get Molly and Mandy back to the menagerie?'

Gracie looked down at her brother's dessert. 'Sorry, George,' she grabbed the fruit and waved it in the air. 'Here,' she called, 'use this to lure them.'

The chimps noticed at once.

Hilda held out her hands like a baseball catcher and Gracie tossed the slippery banana.

George squealed with delight.

Hilda broke the banana in two and threw half to Mr Ramsbottom. The keepers bent their knees in unison and spread their legs, ready to catch the cheeky chimps.

'They look like a couple of gunslingers,' said George. '*Pow, pow.*' He pretended to fire bullets into the air like a cowboy.

'Shush, George,' said Tom.

The chimpanzees looked from keeper to keeper.

The keepers wiggled the banana pieces letting the apes lock on to the scent.

'Come on, Mandy,' called Hilda.

'Come on, Molly,' said Mr Ramsbottom.

'It's working, thank goodness,' said Gracie. The chimps had calmed down at last and were following the keepers.

Tom, Violet and the other diners burst into applause.

'Those chimps are banned from now on,' Lin called out. 'Haven't I got enough to do without a blooming chimp's tea party in here!'

'Oh, get back in the kitchen,' the keeper retorted.

Lin's scowled.

'He's very rude,' said Gracie.

'Yes, he is,' replied Lin. She composed herself. 'Shall I get you a fresh banana?'

George shook his head, 'I feel a bit sick after eating all that ice cream.'

'Well, if you're sure,' replied Lin. 'Is there anything else I can do for you?'

'Actually,' Gracie wiped her sticky fingers on her napkin. 'I noticed you seem a bit short staffed . . . Have you got any vacancies?'

Lin glanced at Gracie's arm.

'I have experience. I waitress in my family's boarding house.'

'We could certainly do with more help,' she passed over her notebook. 'Write down your name and number and I'll give it to Cook, once he's calmed down.'

'Well done, Gracie,' said Tom. 'Working in the Oriental Lounge, you'll be able to spy on the suspects and find out more about them.'

But a few minutes later, Gracie saw the cook staring over at her. He was shaking his head. She was going to have to try and find a job elsewhere.

Chapter Five
The Joke's on George

After they'd finished their desserts and hot chocolate, they made their way out on to the promenade. They agreed to meet up again at The Majestic after tea.

'We'll come down on the tram, we'll get the 252,' said Violet.

Tom rolled his eyes. 'You are such a transport bore, sis.'

'Are we getting the tram home?' asked George. 'Only, I think all that jiggling up and down might make me vomit.'

'Oh, George! I think we'd better get some fresh air and walk.'

There was still an icy wind blowing and Gracie's skin tingled as they walked along the Golden Mile, past its many rock and souvenir shops. Even though Wednesday was half-day closing, many of the tourist shops were still trading.

'Ooh, Jokes Galore,' marvelled George, as they reached a blue-and-yellow-striped store. 'Gags, wigs, tricks, novelties... they've got *everything*!'

'Including itching powder,' said Gracie, pointing at the window display. She checked the sign on the door. Open. 'Let's go in.'

The brass bell above the door rang as they entered the shop. It was crammed full of stuff; shelves groaned under the weight of funny hats, comedy masks and silly props.

The shopkeeper was standing behind a glass counter. He wore a beige overcoat and a pair of oversized glasses with a plastic nose attached.

Gracie took George's hand and they squeezed past a mannequin dressed as Father Christmas. 'Don't . . . touch . . . anything,' she warned him.

'See summat you like?' asked the shopkeeper, wiggling his glasses.

'Look! Pretend poo,' chuckled George. 'We could put it in the toilet at The Majestic.'

'We could *not*,' said Gracie.

The man laughed. 'You have exceptional taste, but are you flush?'

George sniggered.

'We want itching powder,' said Gracie. 'That's all.'

The shopkeeper sighed. 'Well, I need to scratch a living.' He turned and pulled out a small drawer from a tall wooden chest and put it down on the counter.

He pointed to a green tin. 'This is our best seller. People are always itching to buy it.'

'Like a dog with fleas,' added George.

'Exactly,' said the shopkeeper, prising off the lid.

'What's it made from?' asked Gracie. 'It looks like cactus hairs.'

'You're close, miss. Rosehip hairs to be exact.'

'I'll take it.' It was identical to the powder Gracie had found on Natalya's clothing. 'I don't suppose you remember selling any recently?'

The shopkeeper scratched his head. 'Well, all my customers tend to blend into one, unless there's summat unusual about them. I mean I'll remember you . . . because of all the questions,' he hastened.

Gracie put the tin in her shoulder bag and took out her purse. 'And has there been anyone unusual?'

The shopkeeper rubbed a finger against the plastic nose. 'You mean apart from Father Christmas doing some last-minute shopping,' he roared with laughter. 'There's always lots of children in buying it. I sold some to a couple of boys and a girl too. Can't remember what they looked like.'

'Do you get grown-up customers?'

'Oh yes, businessmen love playing pranks on their work colleagues. Let me think, this week I've sold dirty-face soap, snake-in-a-can, spinning bow ties, exploding golf balls, squirting cigarettes . . .'

'Stink bombs?' asked George.

'I *smell* one or two.'

'Sneezing powder?'

'Sales are not to be *sniffed* at.'

George snorted. 'Hand buzzers?'

'You'd be *shocked* how popular they are. Now, is there anything else?'

'I don't think so,' said Gracie.

'Have we enough for a whoopee cushion an' all?' asked George, hopefully. 'You could get it me as a present.'

'Go on then.'

The shopkeeper passed it over. 'You'll come up *trumps* with that, lad.'

George guffawed and shoved the cushion into his trouser pocket.

Chapter Six
Food for Thought

'Oh good, you're home,' called Phyllis from the top of a step ladder in the hallway, as Gracie and George entered The Majestic.

The maid was fastening a length of red and green paper chains across the ceiling.

'That looks very festive. Want a hand?' asked Gracie.

'Yes, please,' replied Phyllis. 'Could you pass me up that next row? I want to create a zigzag effect, and I've been up and down this ladder like a window cleaner.'

Gracie put down her bag, and gently gathered up the crepe decorations. 'Here you are.'

Phyllis quickly secured the rest of the chains, while George held the ladder.

'How was the ballet?' asked Phyllis, as she made her way down the steps.

'Eventful . . .' Gracie then told Phyllis all about the problems at the Blackpool Tower Children's Ballet.

'Gosh!' Phyllis replied, as she folded up the ladder. 'And how will you work out which of the suspects is guilty?' she asked.

'We were hoping to have a spy in the ballet, but I can't dance and neither can Violet. Tom would be great, only they don't allow boys.'

'I can help,' said George.

'Oh, thanks.' Phyllis thrust the ladder to him. 'Be a darling and put it back in the yard for me.'

'What? I didn't mean. Never mind.' He took the ladder's weight and headed down the hallway.

'I can dance,' said Phyllis. 'I could be your spy. I used to go to ballet classes, I've probably still got a leotard, tutu and ballet shoes somewhere, if they still fit.'

'That's great. I'll discuss it with Tom and Violet when they get here.'

'All right, just let me know what I need to do.'

Gracie headed into the kitchen. It was lovely and warm. Ma was stirring a big pot of soup on the stove.

'Is it pea and ham?' asked Gracie, sniffing the air.

'Yes, and don't worry – I made enough for us, too.'

George reappeared from the yard. 'I'm starving, can I have mine now.'

'After the guests, you know the rules,' said Ma. 'And have you fed your pets today?'

'Not yet,' he sighed, jabbing the fire with an iron poker.

'Come on, I'll hold while you refresh the water and food,' said Ma. 'You and Gracie can manage without me, can't you.'

'Of course,' said Phyllis, slicing a loaf while Gracie started to butter.

Mum and George would be a while. George had a rat, two doves, a budgie, a rabbit and a visiting wild seagull to care for.

The dining room was filled with guests, including The Hill sisters – regulars at The Majestic.

'You're doing a grand job, Gracie,' said Edna, peering over the top of her glasses, as Gracie and Phyllis served the sisters.

'You're nearly as quick as Phyllis now,' agreed Elspeth, taking a bread roll.

The sisters sipped at their soup. The meaty aroma was making Gracie's stomach rumble. *Roll on New Year*, she thought. She was looking forward to the guests leaving in January and the novelty of being able to have her own tea at five o'clock instead of having to wait until after the guests had finished.

'Are you enjoying Christmas in Blackpool, ladies?' she asked.

'Oh, yes,' said Edna. 'We're looking forward to our

Christmas dinner and all the trimmings – and we can't wait to find out what surprise you've got lined up for us!'

'*Surprise*?'

Elspeth winked. 'When Mrs Yates ran The Majestic, she always put on a pantomime. Oh, they were funny! I suppose your mother is planning something new, now she's landlady, and you've been keeping it a big secret.'

'Do all the boarding houses put on entertainment at Christmas?' asked Gracie, trying not to sound panicked.

'Oh, yes. Mind you, nothing as grand as the big hotels,' she passed the newspaper over. 'It says The Imperial will have an Elizabethan banquet complete with a boar's head brought to the table in a procession featuring twenty-five Tudor characters!

'The Clifton has a huge model of a castle in snow and a choir will perform a special concert around their Christmas Tree – their dining room is festooned with flowers and holly.'

'There'll be fancy dress balls, whist drives, murder mysteries, ghost storytelling and visits from Father Christmas, naturally,' added Elspeth. 'I can't wait to hear what The Majestic has in store for us! I'm sure it will be a fabulous holiday treat! You *will* let us know if we need to choose costumes, though, won't you? I quite fancy being Little Bo Peep!'

'At your age!' laughed Edna. 'You'd be better off as Old Father Time!'

'I'm sure Ma is planning something lovely,' said Gracie.

Her mind reeling as she stepped away from their table. Pantomimes! Fancy dress! Why had no one mentioned earlier that they were supposed to put on a festive show! Poor Ma!

She followed Phyllis back into the kitchen. The maid put on oven gloves and opened the oven door to take out a large dish of apple crumble.

Gracie tried not to think about the mountain of dishes that would need doing, and then she'd have to help Phyllis set the dining-room for breakfast. If she could find a well paid new winter job, perhaps she could persuade Ma to let her do less at home. After all being a landlady wasn't her dream. Perhaps it was time she worked out what was.

Gracie put *The Gazette* on the kitchen table and had a quick flick through. The paper was packed with advertisements for pantomimes, dance bands, concerts, film screenings and gala dances. The Opera House, the Grand Theatre, the Winter Gardens and the Palace all had a packed schedule, while the Tower had the *Cirque d'Hiver*, the Children's Ballet and a boxing match. There was even a Boxing Day dog show! Perhaps she could find a job with one of them? She turned to the recruitment vacancies, but there were only two; one for a milkman and one for an engineer.

'I've been thinking,' said Phyllis. 'If you're going to interview lots of suspects, you need to write everything down. You should get one of them reporter's notebooks.'

'A reporter's – oh, that gives me an idea.' Gracie leant over and planted a kiss on her cheek. 'You're a genius!'

'You look like the cat that's got the cream,' said Phyllis.

'The custard actually,' said Gracie, lifting the jug and pouring it over the crumble.

* * *

Violet and Tom arrived about an hour later. Ma let them use the kitchen, while she read a book in the communal parlour.

The Embertons took off their rucksacks and placed them under the table, then sat down next to George who was writing a Christmas list.

Gracie offered to make Ovaltine for everyone and warmed a pan of milk on the stove.

Violet read over George's shoulder. 'What do you want this year?'

'What *isn't* he asking for! He keeps changing his mind,' said Gracie, rolling her eyes. 'Don't come wailing to me if Father Christmas ends up very confused and brings you the wrong thing.'

'I *have* decided on summat,' said George. 'I want a cannon, with real cannonballs.'

'A *cannon*?' repeated Tom. 'I think Father Christmas's elves might struggle to make one of those. Why don't you ask for a pop gun instead?'

'I want something big . . . Oh! But how will Father

Christmas know where to bring my presents now we've moved to Blackpool?'

'You'll have to write to him – tell him you've moved,' said Gracie. 'You could send the letter up the chimney!'

'Or you could give him your letter in person,' said Violet.

George guffawed. 'How would I get to the North Pole?'

'You don't need to,' said Tom. 'Father Christmas is coming to Blackpool! He always gives out the presents at the Blackpool Tower Christmas Eve Party.'

'*Really*? That's terrific!'

'Want to know what else is terrific?' asked Gracie. 'Phyllis says she could be our ballet spy.'

'Fantastic,' said Tom.

'Isn't it!'

'We have news too,' said Violet. 'We're going to be away for a couple of days. We're going to visit our Gran. We don't see her very often,' she continued quietly. 'Not since Ma died.'

'We're getting the train to Yorkshire in the morning,' added Tom.

'That's nice,' said Gracie. 'Do you think you could do me a favour before you leave?'

'What is it?' asked Violet.

'You know I've been after a new job. For the winter, like . . .'

'Go on,' said Violet.

Gracie opened a cupboard and took out the tin of Ovaltine

and scooped the powder into four mugs. 'Well . . . I was hoping you could get me one. It was Phyllis that gave me the idea actually . . . do you think your Pa could get me a trial as a reporter at *The Gazette*?'

'A reporter?' said Tom.

'It would be the ideal way to question suspects at the Tower. I'd have to persuade Ma too, of course.' She poured the milk into the mugs.

'We'll ask him when we get home,' said Violet. 'We'll ring you later.'

'Great!' Gracie sat down.

'*PPPPTTTHHHMMMPP!!!*' A loud farting noise erupted from under her bottom.

She turned bright red. 'George!'

Her brother roared with laughter. 'Got you! Got you!'

Gracie stood up and removed the whoopee cushion from under the padded seat. 'I thought this was for Christmas?'

'I said it was a present, I didn't say a *Christmas* present,' sniggered George into his mug.

She threw the whoopee cushion at him and chased him out of the room.

Chapter Seven

The Five Ws

'So, you want to be a reporter,' said Mr Emberton the next morning, as he welcomed Gracie at *The Gazette*'s reception. 'A noble pursuit. A journalist always seeks the truth. Without fear or favour,' he emphasised, pointing at *The Gazette*'s motto above the desk. 'Do you know what that means, Gracie?'

'Not really,' she replied, smiling nervously at Violet and Tom's dad.

'Without fear or favour means you mustn't be afraid to write a story and that you shouldn't be persuaded not to publish it, nor should you be pressurised into writing one because it unfairly benefits someone,' replied Mr Emberton. 'You might get asked about that. They call it ethics.'

Gracie raised her eyebrows, after all, Mr Emberton had kept the story about the attempted Illuminations Switch-On theft out of the papers. Perhaps publicists worked to different rules than journalists.

Mr Emberton led the way down a long wood-panelled corridor. The noise of clattering typewriters grew louder and louder. 'After you,' he said, as he swung open a pair of double doors. The sound was even louder, and joined now by chatter. There was a strong smell of ink, cigarettes and coffee.

The newsroom was a big open room with shiny lino flooring and groups of polished wooden desks. It was a hive of activity; everyone seemed to know exactly what to do.

Gracie hoped she fitted in. She had put on her best white blouse and a knee-length tweed skirt. Ma had lent her a pair of black shoes with a modest heel. She'd felt very grown up getting dressed, but now she felt very young.

'Here we have the reporters . . .' explained Mr Emberton. There were seven men and two women grouped together in the centre of the room. There were seven men grouped together in the centre of the room. They were dressed in suits and ties.

Three of the men were poised over notebooks filled with strange squiggles, two more were furiously hitting the keys of their big black, metal typewriters, while the remaining men and women were on the phone. 'We have six dedicated telephone lines. This new office has all mod cons, including flushing toilets!'

Gracie swallowed. Could she really find the courage to do what these people did? Speaking to strangers, asking them questions they might not like, then writing up the words for all of Blackpool to read?

Mr Emberton pointed to another set of desks where a group of eight grizzly looking older men were smoking furiously. 'That's the sub-editors, they check the copy for errors and legalities – they make sure everything is spelt correctly and that no one has written something that will put the editor in jail.'

'Sport . . .' whispered Mr Emberton. Men again, mixed ages, in the middle of a debate about the upcoming boxing match. 'Their choice of language is not suited to a lady's presence. Steer clear.'

Gracie nodded.

'I'd suggest you sit with Features,' he walked her to a smaller, exceptionally tidy bank of desks.

'This is Ava.'

A woman with a perfectly straight brown bob, dressed in a lilac blouse with a pussy cat bow, smiled. 'And what's your name, sweetheart?' she asked, as she put fresh paper into her typewriter.

'Gracie Fairshaw.'

'And you want to be a reporter?' asked Ava.

She'd prepared an answer to the question. She held the woman's gaze. 'Yes, I enjoyed English in school, and I like finding out about people.' She hoped she sounded more confident than she felt.

'That will help, but journalism isn't for everyone, and it's particularly challenging for girls.' She lowered her voice. 'Some of the men here think we should stick to the kitchen or raising babies.'

'Fortunately, Mr Grime is far more forward-thinking,' said Mr Emberton, before guiding Gracie towards an office door marked EDITOR. 'The Grimes *are The Gazette*.'

Gracie's stomach filled with butterflies as Mr Emberton knocked on the door.

'Come in,' hollered a gruff voice.

They entered the room. It was all leather and pipe smoke. The wall was covered with awards and photographs of the man behind the desk with a host of well-known faces. There were film stars, sporting heroes and even the Prime Minister.

'Ah, Emberton, is this our new cub reporter?' Mr Grime got up and held out his hand. He had a smartly trimmed white beard and friendly hazel eyes.

Cub? thought Gracie. *I sound like a young bear!*

She shook his hand. 'I'm Gracie Fairshaw.'

'Indeed! Charmed to meet you. Please sit down . . .'

Gracie straightened her back.

'Mr Emberton speaks very highly of you. But, of course, I need to assess if you have what it takes, *Miss* Fairshaw, to be a journalist?' said Mr Grime, smoothing his mustard-coloured tie.

Her stomach felt wishy-washy. 'Yes, sir.'

'Excellent. I want you to write 500 words on what children are hoping Father Christmas will bring them.' He pulled open a drawer and threw a notebook at her.

Gracie caught it with ease.

Mr Grime beamed. 'We should put you on our cricket team in the summer. Now, Gracie, tell me, do you know how to write in shorthand?'

Gracie frowned. *Was that what those strange squiggles had been?*

Mr Emberton stepped in. 'Ava could teach her, but she can manage without for now – we all have to at first.'

The editor roared with laughter. 'Quite! You'll need to type up your copy too. I'll give you until half-past ten.'

'Yes, sir,' replied Gracie, her head reeling. *Was 500 words a lot? It sounded a lot, and what was copy?*

'Oh, and one last tip, before you go,' said Mr Grime. 'Always keep your eyes peeled for a story!'

Gracie nodded and followed Mr Emberton back into the newsroom, clasping her new notebook tightly.

She took a seat on the features desk. There was a sharp-looking stick, a typewriter still in its cover and a telephone.

'That's your spike,' said Ava, 'you stab any completed press releases on it.' She waved her own spike at Gracie. It was full of pierced paper. Ava must write an awful lot of stories.

'Mr Grime wondered if you could give Gracie some shorthand lessons,' said Mr Emberton.

'Of course,' replied Ava. 'We'll start you slowly, don't worry, we're not expecting you to reach 130 words per minute overnight. I've got a book you can borrow that covers the basics, and I can run through some of the exercises with you.'

'Thank you.' George would be jealous! Shorthand was like writing in code.

'Can you type?'

Gracie lifted her chin. 'Yes. A little. My Pa had a typewriter, and he used to let me play with it. I used to like making up stories on it.' They still had the typewriter, though Pa now lived in Wales with his new family. 'I'm not very quick though.'

'You'll have to be, reporters are expected to type eighty words per minute!'

'Gosh!' she wiggled her fingers, imaging them trying to hit the required speed. She would have to work twice as hard as everyone else.

'You'll soon get the hang of it. Practice makes perfect.' Ava smiled and lowered her voice. 'What's your first assignment?'

'I've got to write 500 words about the most popular toys this Christmas.'

'So, who might be able to tell you that?' asked Ava. 'You need a source. An expert.'

Gracie's mind flashed back to last Christmas. A memory of

their Milltown home. Opening presents with George, in front of a roaring fire. A small Christmas tree in the corner, decorated with electric candles. They hadn't bought a tree for The Majestic yet, but they could get a big one for the boarding house parlour. What toys might be wrapped and waiting under it this year?

'How about a toy shop?' offered Ava, bringing Gracie out of her daydream. 'You'll find the telephone numbers for a few listed in here.' She passed over a directory.

'Thank you.' Gracie flicked through the listings, steadying the book with her left elbow. She looked down the names of Blackpool businesses for a toy shop. She recognised one of the names – Lakin's Toy Shop. She'd passed it many a time, and it was close to *The Gazette*'s office.

Gracie's hand shook as she reached out for the telephone. She hooked the receiver under her chin and dialled the number.

She bit her bottom lip as the ringing tone began.

Gracie heard a click as the call was answered. 'Good morning. Lakin's Toys, Blackpool 6153, Ted Lakin speaking.'

Gracie took a deep breath. 'Hello, Mr Lakin. This is Miss Gracie Fairshaw from *The Gazette*,' she said enthusiastically. 'I'm writing a feature on this Christmas's most popular toys . . .'

'I see,' replied Mr Lakin cautiously. 'Well, we could do with some publicity in the run up to Christmas . . .'

'I have some questions to ask you. Erm . . .' She felt her cheeks burning. She couldn't think of a single one. 'But it would be better if I could speak to you in person. Can I come over to the shop now?'

'Well, yes, we are a bit quiet at the moment,' said Mr Lakin.

'Great. I'll be with you in fifteen minutes. Goodbye!' Gracie put down the phone and sighed.

'Hey, what's the matter?' asked Ava kindly. 'You did really well. You've got your first interview lined up.'

'But I have no idea what questions to ask,' whispered Gracie.

'That's easy. Just remember the five Ws.'

'But I've never even heard of the five Ws,' said Gracie, a tremble in her voice.

'They're really simple. Who, Where, What, When and Why.'

'Oh,' said Gracie, smiling, 'That works for mystery solving too.'

'And don't worry about the time. When you get back, you read out your story and I'll type it up. Then we'll show Mr Grime. Us girls have to stick together. Now, let's go and find Dennis, you'll want him to take a photo of Mr Lakin in his shop.'

They made their way over to the photographers' desks.

'We'll need him to take some shots of you, an' all, Gracie,' said Ava, nodding at one of the men with grey hair.

Chapter Eight
Toy Shop

Gracie looked up at the Lakin's Toys sign that swung gently in the sea breeze. The old-fashioned Victorian-style lettering was worn, and the shop paintwork was peeling in places.

The shop window needed a clean, and a few dusty pieces of old holly made a forlorn border around the glass. The centrepiece of the display was a large, sun-bleached dolls' house, complete with tiny furniture. Mucky-faced porcelain dolls and faded teddy bears looked back at Gracie.

Dennis lifted his press camera. She had only ever seen one in Hollywood movies at the picture house.

The photographer pressed a button on top so the front hinged down, revealing the lens. Then he pulled out the camera with its bellows and secured it in position. Finally, he attached the large flash bulb on the side.

Gracie pushed open the door and stepped inside. A little bell tinkled overhead.

The shelves were filled with dusty-looking boxes, and there were no customers. A large table in the centre of the shop was set out with special offers; there were some building blocks, a few spinning tops, a couple of faded puppets and some lead toy soldiers.

She took a deep breath and called over to the teenage boy behind the wooden cash desk. He looked positively bored as he cast a yo-yo up and down. 'I'm looking for Mr Lakin. I'm here to interview him for *The Gazette.*' She hoped her nerves didn't show.

'He's in the back,' the boy waved a finger towards a door the back of the shop.

'Ladies first,' said Dennis. They pushed their way past tall shelves filled with grubby jigsaws and shabby-looking board games.

The door led to a short corridor. A sole light bulb hung from the ceiling. She brushed away a cobweb.

She peered into the first room on the left. It was a stockroom; jammed full of more dirty, squashed boxes. 'Mr Lakin?' she called. 'It's Gracie Fairshaw. We spoke on the phone.'

'In here!'

She spun around. A man's head appeared from a door on the right. He had grey curly hair and pale blue eyes behind gold-rimmed spectacles.

'You're a bit young for a reporter, aren't you?' He pushed his glasses nearer to his eyes. 'Why, you're no older than my grandchild! Still, everyone seems young at my age.' He beckoned her nearer.

They went into a small back office that smelt of egg.

Mr Lakin sat down next to a round table and indicated for Gracie to do the same. Dennis hovered at her shoulder. There was a stack of boxes piled on the floor.

A partially eaten sandwich was on the table next to an open ledger.

Gracie placed her notebook on the table and took out a pencil. She rested her left elbow on the pad to stop it moving as she wrote.

Who? she thought.

'Can I check your name, please?'

'Edward Lakin, but folk call me Ted.'

'And that's L – A – K . . .'

'I, N, yes,' finished Mr Lakin.

'And how old are you?'

'Sixty – and I feel it.'

She didn't know what to say. What was the next W? *Where.* 'And what's your address, please.'

'Here, I live above the shop.'

She jotted down Lakin's Toy Shop, Church Street.' *When*. 'And have you worked here for a long time?'

He wrapped his thumbs around his braces. 'Forty-four years.'

'I noticed you have a lovely dolls' house in the window,' commented Gracie.

'Yes.'

She frowned. It wasn't much of an answer.

Mr Lakin picked up one of the boxes and blew the dust off it, revealing a faded picture of a steam locomotive. He took a pencil and reduced the price on the old label.

She tried again.

'Have you been busy? Lots of sales?'

'No,' replied Mr Lakin.

Dennis leant over and whispered in her ear. 'You need to ask open questions.'

'Open?' she asked.

'Ones that you can't answer "yes" or "no" to.'

She concentrated. The five Ws were open questions. 'WHAT are your best sellers this year?' asked Gracie.

The shopkeeper gave a short, bitter laugh.

'Perhaps if you tell me some of the items that you'd like to sell, I could feature them in the article.

Ted Lakin nodded. 'Sorry, you're right. Well, I'm discounting these model trains and I could reduce the price on the smaller boxes of Meccano. I'm hoping for a delivery of interlocking Minibrix and tin soldiers, but the fog's held up the order.'

'My friend Violet loves Meccano,' added Gracie, trying to brighten the mood. 'She's always borrowing her brother's set.'

Mr Lakin cocked his head to one side. 'Really? I've got a bit behind with trends.' He lowered his voice conspiratorially. 'I did read something in the trade press about a new board game in America where you buy up houses. Britain's farm and zoo animals never go out of fashion, and jigsaws are always popular.

'Of course, dolls are always a favourite with girls. I've had a couple of mothers buying lots of those paper dolls; you dress them in paper clothes!

'The only problem is the complaints when they fall apart. Kids nowadays play too rough; they're always breaking things in my shop. When I was young, children had good manners. They would always say "please" and "thank you".'

'What is your number-one seller?' asked Gracie, trying to change the subject.

'Mickey,' said Mr Lakin, adjusting his glasses again. 'They'll buy anything with that mouse on it. Luckily, I've got a few old annuals in stock.'

Gracie jotted down some final comments, then they went

into the shop so Dennis could take some photographs of Mr Lakin and the toys.

'Are you going to take today's letters with you?' asked Mr Lakin as he posed next to a wooden castle.

'Letters?' asked Gracie, blinking as the flash went off.

Mr Lakin pointed to a large cardboard letter box, painted red. 'It was Auntie Astra's idea. Parents bring their children into the shop so they can write their letter to Father Christmas. Then they post them in the special letter box. The letters get passed on to *The Gazette*, who print some of them on the children's page.

'That way, Father Christmas and parents know what the children are hoping for,' he said. 'I just wish children nowadays weren't so demanding. In my day it was, 'I'd like' and not 'I want.' Some children are in here every day posting a new letter! I tell them, "remember Father Christmas only brings presents to good children." There's a few kids I'd only give a lump of coal to!'

'While Gracie collects the letters, can we get a photo of you behind the counter?' asked Dennis.

'Go on then,' said Mr Lakin.

Gracie opened the back of the letter box and reached inside. She could feel several envelopes. She scooped them up. There were about a dozen in all. She pulled them out and dropped them into her shoulder bag. Then she spotted one more on the

floor. It wasn't in an envelope and the apricot-coloured paper had been trodden on. Gracie hated the idea of someone's wishes not being read so she added it to the pile.

'I need to take some of you too, Gracie,' said Dennis, aiming his camera at her. 'Smile for the birdie!'

Chapter Nine

A Letter to Father Christmas

Gracie clutched her notebook as she glanced up at *The Gazette*'s octagonal clock. It was ten o'clock already! She had half an hour to write up her story. Her mind whirred, could she really hit her deadline? Gracie began to run, pounding up the outside steps and into the brand-new building. She sprang down the corridor and into the bustling newsroom.

Gracie sat and began to write up her notes. Chewing on her pencil as she struggled to find the right words.

She crossed out her introductory paragraph and tried again.

'Use the five Ws,' Ava reminded her. 'Who, where . . .'

She tried again. *A Blackpool shopkeeper* . . . Hmm, that was OK, but Mr Grime wanted the article to be about what children wanted – that would work better.

The words started to flow.

She glanced at the clock. She was running out of time.

'Don't worry. You read, I'll type,' said Ava, poised over her typewriter.

Gracie dictated her notes. She hoped she had made Lakin's Toy Shop sound more festive than it had felt. 'Children across Blackpool have written . . .'

Ava banged away at the typewriter keys, the metal bars striking against the ribbon, printing Gracie's words on to a crisp sheet of paper. *Clack, clack, clack.*

'. . . their letters to Father Christmas . . .'

The typewriter dinged at the end of the line and Ava pushed the carriage return back into position for the next line.

'. . . and this year, good little boys and girls are hoping for a mouse! No! Not a real one . . .'

Ding!

'. . . but the popular cartoon character, Mickey Mouse!'

'That's great! You're a natural,' said Ava. 'Keep going.'

Gracie grinned with pride. 'Ted Lakin, 60, has run Lakin's Toy Shop on Church Street for over forty years. Entering this traditional toy shop is like stepping back in time. Families will find exploring the small family-run shop a real Christmas treat, with bygone favourites, and classic toys that never go out of fashion, available for all pockets.'

Gracie and Ava found a natural rhythm as they finished the article together.

'Well done,' said Ava, pulling the paper out of the typewriter. 'You'd better file your copy with Mr Grime.'

Gracie's legs felt wobbly as she took her first news story from Ava. Every footstep seemed extra loud as she walked across to the editor's office. Would he like her story? Was it good enough to be printed? She tucked the paper under her left arm and knocked quietly on Mr Grime's door.

'Come in!'

Mr Grime was sitting at his desk, puffing on his pipe. 'Excellent! You made your deadline, and with five minutes to spare!' He held out his hand and Gracie gave him her story.

She felt all jittery as the editor read. It seemed to take for ever, and Mr Grime's facial expression gave little away. Occasionally he nodded or took the pencil from behind his ear to make an amendment. She crossed her fingers behind her back.

'Not bad,' said Mr Grime, stroking his white beard. 'In fact, rather good.' He reached into his desk drawer. 'Congratulations, Miss Fairshaw, you are officially a journalist.'

Gracie burst into a smile. 'Thank you, sir. Does that mean you're going to use it in the paper?'

'It does indeed. It will make a nice lead story in tonight's edition.' He checked the clock. 'The paper is put to bed at 1pm; your story will need checking and pasting up.' He stood up and opened his door, wafting Gracie's copy. 'Subs! I've got something for that gap on page seven.'

One of the men dashed over and took her story from Mr Grime. 'Give our new reporter a byline. Gracie Fairshaw – F, A, I, R, S, H, A, W.'

The man nodded and hurried back to his desk.

'We don't put bylines on every story, you know,' said Mr Grime, as they went back into his office, 'just the ones that are a bit special, or important.'

'Thank you, sir.' Gracie grinned again. She could picture Ma flicking through the paper after tea and spotting the byline. She'd be really surprised.

Mr Grime checked his pocket watch. 'Ten thirty. Right, Gracie, I'd like you to meet the most important person at *The Gazette*.'

Gracie wrinkled her brow; she thought that was the editor. She followed Mr Grime back into the newsroom.

Phone calls were halted, cigarettes stubbed out, typewriting stopped, conversations ended. Everyone had stopped work. The newsroom fell silent as they turned their heads towards a distant door.

The only sound was a squeak and a jingly rattle. An old

woman in an apron pushed a metal tea trolley into the room, and towards the editor.

'The place would fall apart without our Rosie,' said Mr Grime, as the tea lady positioned her trolley in front of him. 'She keeps us fed and watered, and she hears all the gossip.'

Rosie laughed, as she poured from a large metal teapot.

'What sweet treat have you got for me today?' asked Mr Grime.

'Victoria sponge, sir.'

'Ah, my favourite. And a piece for our newest recruit, Miss Gracie Fairshaw, too, please Rosie.'

'Right-o, sir.'

Gracie returned to her desk while tea and cake was handed out.

Rosie placed a mug of strong tea and a slice of jammy sponge cake in front of Gracie. She took a big bite and sipped her tea. She was slowly beginning to feel part of the team.

Mr Emberton and Ava strolled over to the features desk, each carrying a mug of tea and a Chocolate Crisp.

'I hear you're off to a flying start,' said Mr Emberton, sitting in a spare chair.

Gracie smiled. 'Thanks to Ava.'

'Nonsense,' said Ava, tearing the foil on her chocolate. 'You earned that byline.'

'I don't suppose you've any idea what *my* children would like for Christmas,' said Mr Emberton.

'Tom likes anything to do with music and dance,' said Gracie. 'And Violet would love a model train.'

Mr Emberton laughed. 'Don't worry, Father Christmas knows not to bring dolls for my daughter. I wonder if Tom would like a drum?'

'You'll have to get them to send Father Christmas a letter,' teased Gracie. 'Oh, I nearly forgot, Mr Lakin asked me to pass you the latest batch.' She reached into her shoulder bag for them.

'Oh, thanks Gracie, that will save me a trip. Actually, I'm behind with Auntie Astra's page. I don't suppose you could read through those letters you collected and pick out a couple of interesting ones for me to include?'

'I'd be happy to,' said Gracie. She was enjoying being given different tasks to do. It certainly made a change from stripping beds and serving up meals.

* * *

Once she'd finished her drink, Gracie turned her attention to the Father Christmas letters. She took each letter in turn. They had already been opened; the telltale tear from a metal letter opener was along the edge.

Mr Lakin must sneak a peek at them first, she thought. *That way he can be sure to have his shop stocked with the presents on every wish list of Blackpool's boys and girls.*

Gracie pulled out the first letter from its envelope.

Dear Father Christmas,

I didn't mean to cut my sister's hair. I am very sorry. Please can I still have a toy boat for Christmas, and can you give Lucy new plaits.

Yours sincerely

Danny Roberts

Gracie giggled. She put it to one side and opened the next letter.

Dear Father Christmas,

I hope you are not too busy getting ready to deliver all the toys. I can't wait for you to visit my house. I will leave out some carrots for the reindeer and a mince pie and glass of milk for you. Please do not use the chimney as I am worried you will get stuck. I would like a Mickey Mouse for Christmas, one that I can cuddle at bedtime.

Thank you very much.

Christine

It was a nice letter and it had just the right tone for Auntie Astra's page.

Gracie opened the rest of the letters; they were all from children asking politely for a toy. Mickey Mouse was mentioned in most, with requests for yo-yos, drums, xylophones, colouring books, crayons and paint boxes featuring the character, as well as more traditional teddy bears, dolls, tin cars and wooden fire engines.

Gracie set them aside and read the final letter. It was the one without an envelope. A muddy black footprint had been trodden across the apricot-coloured paper, but she could just about decipher it.

Dear Father Christmas,

I know I'm probably too old to be writing to you, but you're the only person who can help.

I don't want a toy for Christmas, what I want more than anything is to be a ballerina. The prima dancer.

I have been practising my steps over and over. I'd do ANYTHING to be a ballet star like Margot Fonteyn. I am ready.

The bottom of the paper was torn, and the name was missing. She supposed there were hundreds of girls in Blackpool who wanted to be ballerinas.

* * *

Mr Grime exited his office and headed towards the features desk. Gracie put Christine's letter and one asking for a growling teddy bear to the top of the pile and marked them as suitable for Auntie Astra's page.

'So, Miss Fairshaw, are you ready for another special assignment?' he asked.

'Yes, sir.'

'I want you to go over to the Tower tomorrow. Ava usually writes our entertainment reviews, but I thought it would be more original to have a young person write about *Winter Belles*, the Children's Ballet Christmas Show this year. Your name will be on the press list for the matinee performance.' Mr Grime lowered his voice. 'The show starts at 2pm.'

'Thank you.' This was better than she'd hoped. Mr Grime was giving her the perfect excuse to snoop around and quiz the dancers properly.

Chapter Ten
Nose Dive

Gracie felt very important giving her name to the Tower concierge who checked her off on his list of guests. She clasped her complimentary programme and ticket tightly and made her way to the staircase.

The Children's Ballet was a popular attraction with families and there was quite a queue leading up to the ballroom. A sense of anticipation was building – young girls practised their ballet positions on the steps, while their mothers scolded them to be careful in case they fell. She was nervous in crowds, so Gracie distracted herself by looking at the blue wall tiles depicting birds and fishes.

As she stood waiting, someone barged into her. Gracie turned to see the back of a woman in a brown fur coat with a thick, upright collar. She was pushing her way through to the front.

A commotion followed in her trail. The woman's voice was raised. The crowd budged up to eavesdrop.

Gracie leant around the queue. 'I've looked everywhere else,' said the woman, grabbing the usher's arm. 'Please let me check inside. She might have sneaked past you while you've been checking tickets.'

'I'm sorry, madam, but I'm under strict instructions not to let anyone into the ballroom before 2 p.m.'

'Don't you know who I am?' The woman sighed. '*Please*, I need to find my mother.'

The man folded his arms.

The doors to the ballroom were opened from the inside.

'Now you may enter,' said the usher, giving a forced smile.

The woman scurried forward, while the rest of the queue moved slowly. At last Gracie was inside the ballroom. She gave a sigh of relief and felt her body relax.

Rows of seats had been set out across the dance floor. The woman in the fur coat stood at the back, scanning them all. Then she twisted on her heels and snaked around the incoming audience.

Gracie checked her ticket and found her seat in the front row. She opened her programme; a change of cast had been pasted over the original listings. *Poor Audrey,* she thought.

Fredini and his dance band – dressed identically in smart

evening suits with black bow-ties – were settling into position below the stage. Fredini was adjusting the height of his microphone.

Gracie had been expecting to see Harry Linnet at the piano but there was a different musician in his spot, and it was a grand piano, not the basic instrument used at the Children's Ballet rehearsal. She wondered where he was.

Gracie placed her notebook on her lap and twiddled her pencil.

Fredini ran a hand over his sleek Brylcreemed hair. 'One two. One two.' His London accent was loud and clear over the microphone. He nodded in satisfaction then went to adjust the position of a large capital 'F' behind the band.

The brass section was standing in a row, the light reflecting off their shining instruments. The trombonist pursed his lips and tested his slide, while the three saxophonists and two trumpeters wiggled their fingers before running through some jazzy scales. Another musician plucked the thick strings of a double bass, checking it was in tune.

The drummer joined in and played a roll on his snare, while his foot beat out a steady rhythm on the bass drum. Next to him was a huge copper kettle drum and something that looked like a giant xylophone but with metal, not wooden, bars.

Gracie leant her notebook in the crook of her left elbow and began to write. She started with a few descriptive words about the set design. She tucked her pencil behind her ear and wondered how much longer it would be until the show started.

She turned her head to see the last of the audience arriving. She wondered if Audrey would come to watch the ballet, or if she was too upset.

'Mother!'

Gracie turned to see the woman in the fur coat fling her arms around an old woman with white hair.

Fredini and his band launched into an overture. Gracie checked her programme, it was a version of Prokofiev's 'Troika', with lots of pretty, jingling sleigh bells.

The audience murmured in anticipation as the lights began to dim. It would be too dark for writing notes; she'd have to rely on her memory and the programme.

She glanced back at the woman in the fur coat – she was helping the old woman out of her long black raincoat. Underneath she was wearing a mismatched blouse decorated with daisies and a skirt covered with triangles, topped off with a multi-coloured knitted hat and evening gloves. She looked rather eccentric.

The younger woman took off her fur coat, revealing a beautiful sparkly blue dress with puff sleeves. Gracie suddenly felt rather drab in her tartan skirt and white jumper.

She felt a thrill of anticipation as the curtains opened. The stage was brilliant white, and a huge fabric backdrop made it look like there were snowy hills in the distance.

A dozen dancers, dressed in short green dresses with lots of fringing, shimmied on to the stage from the wings. Gracie thought they looked like miniature Christmas trees.

The band segued into a jazzy version of 'Winter Wonderland'. Gracie smiled and tapped her foot along to the music.

Potential words for her review filled her head, *'The girls danced in perfect synchronicity, their dresses shimmering with their frenetic movements.'*

The girls formed two rows on either side of the stage, and the music blended into a swinging version of 'Jingle Bells'.

Another small group of girls entered from the stage wings. This time they wore metallic leotards and tutus embroidered with tiny silver bells.

Gracie understood now why hundreds of girls auditioned every year for a chance to be in the Children's Ballet. It wasn't the money – though being from working class homes, the girls' families would be grateful for every penny – no, it was how everyone had their part to play in creating something magical. The Ballet made you forget your troubles and filled your heart with hope for a better future.

A spotlight shone on the girls, who parted to reveal a single girl dressed in gold . . . Ruth.

She seemed to float across the stage, her feet fluttering in perfect time with the music.

Gracie knew nothing about ballet, but she could see why Madame Petrova had chosen her to replace Audrey.

More words for her review came to mind. *'New to her role, 12-year-old Ruth Linnet has a confidence that belies her young age. Dressed in a golden star costume, the Children Ballet's replacement first soloist is mesmerising, with a luminescence that will see her shine in an assured future stage career.'*

At the end of her solo, Ruth stood perfectly still in the centre of the stage and soaked up the applause, her eyes glistening. Gracie clapped her hand against her left arm, enthusiastically.

The stage lights dimmed and the curtain fell so the set could be quickly changed for the second act. The audience chatted happily until a hush signalled the start of 'The Santa Claus Express'.

When the curtain lifted, Frances and a dozen girls were dressed as engine drivers, complete with sooty faces. The band began to play a rhythmic tune and Fredini leant into the microphone . . . '*Choo choo.*'

They formed a conga line, rotating their arms to mimic the motion of a steam train as they tap danced around the stage. They were good, but they didn't have Ruth's star quality.

There was a small disturbance behind her. Gracie turned her head to see Mr Linnet pushing along the row. He waved at the fur coat woman and her older companion, as he tried to reach the empty seat next to them.

The curtain fell.

Gracie checked her programme. They would be changing the set for the third act. The audience chatted and rustled sweet wrappers. Had they saved the best for last?

* * *

The audience applauded as the stage curtains opened to reveal a giant toy shop. Gracie oohed with pleasure.

A painted backdrop depicted shelves filled with teddy bears, porcelain dolls, spinning tops, train sets and clockwork animals.

There was Violet's toy box, as well as a rocking horse, Father Christmas's sleigh and a newly added line of seven Russian nesting dolls in ever decreasing sizes - from giant to tiny!

Dozens of dancers, girls of all ages and sizes in peach leotards and tutus, pooled on to the stage, their arms spread out, holding wing-like fine lace. The sequins on their costumes twinkled under the spotlights as they spun round and round, giving the effect of a swirling blizzard against the glass.

Gracie noticed a sudden movement at the side of the stage.

One extra dancer, with scruffy short brown hair, skidded on to stage clutching a too-big tutu at the waist, her snowflake lace all in a tangle. She joined the back of the chorus, red-faced. Gracie did a double take. Wait, that face . . . could it be? She paled and slid down in her seat. It wasn't a girl at all!

'George!' she breathed.

Gracie shuddered as her brother attempted to copy the other dancers' graceful steps. He exaggerated all the poses and positions, flinging his arms around like a demented gibbon.

He stumbled into the end of the line, knocking them like dominoes. They glared at him, and the girl nearest kicked him in the shin. George thumped her back.

The audience sniggered.

George blew a raspberry at them.

Gracie closed her eyes and prayed no one would find out he was her brother! She subtly gestured with her hand for him to get off stage. But he hadn't even spotted her.

Fredini's voice echoed out, amplified by the microphone. 'In this modern age, children often wonder – how does Father Christmas deliver all his presents in one night? The answer is simple – by aeroplane!' He waved his arm upwards.

A large wooden aircraft swung out from the wing. It was suspended high up near the ceiling by a crane-like metal arm.

Everyone oohed in amazement as it glided over the stage.

Gracie could see someone in red was sitting in the pilot seat. It was Natalya.

'Is that you Santa Claus?' called Fredini.

The audience cheered.

The ballerina waved from up above. 'Ho, ho, ho,' she called. 'Have you been good boys and girls?' She sprinkled snow on to the stage below.

Frances and Ruth stepped on to stage dressed as clouds with trailing snow, they spun around and around underneath the aeroplane.

The rig holding it *looked* strong enough, but as it twisted round further, Gracie heard an ominous creaking sound.

She turned to see if Fredini had heard it too. 'Watch out! Santa's coming in to land . . .'

The plane swivelled. The audience applauded.

The plane's nose dipped.

Gracie checked the dancers' faces. They were all relaxed and smiling. Waving up at Natalya as she sprinkled more snow.

Frances and Ruth still floating around below her.

TWANG! Something barely visible flared. There was the sound of a taut wire snapping. Gracie gripped her arm rest in horror.

The dancers ran back, stumbling and colliding.

Natalya screamed as the aeroplane lurched; its nose dropped sharply.

'George!' cried Gracie.

Chapter Eleven

Hanging in Suspense

Frances and Ruth screamed and scrambled back. Girls ran to the wings, others stood dumbstruck at the rear of the stage, staring up at the plane in horror.

'Get me down, get me down,' cried Natayla, as another wire pinged.

Fredini ran up the stage steps and tugged at a thick rope, the stage curtains falling to conceal the stage. There were more screams from the audience. Gracie turned to see parents covering their children's eyes. Others were pushing their way out of the rows or clambering over seats.

There's going to be a crush, she thought. Everyone was pushing, shoving; trying to get out.

Except the old woman in the mismatched outfit, who

suddenly twisted round and was now racing towards the stage. The fur coat woman called after her, 'Mother!' Then she and Mr Linnet turned about and hared after her.

The band had scooped up their instruments and joined the melee. *Why was no one taking control?* Gracie looked at Fredini's abandoned microphone. She knew what she must do!

She ran to it, swallowed hard and addressed the room. Wincing at the loudness of her voice, she said, 'Ladies and Gentlemen. Boys and Girls. Your attention please.'

People turned their heads towards her. 'There is no need for panic. You are completely safe.'

They hesitated.

'Please return to your seats.'

'My girls!' called the white-haired woman.

Gracie could see terror in her eyes. Of course, she must be Mrs Waters and the fur coat woman must be Little Miri. 'Don't worry, the dancers are all safe,' she soothed, not knowing if that was true. Still, she hadn't heard any awful crashing sound.

'Nora, come and sit by the piano, where it's safe,' said Mr Linnet, steering her away.

'Yes, Harry. What shall I play?'

'I'll tell you in a moment.' He placed a comforting hand on her shoulder, then strode off towards the stage, sprinting up the steps and ducking under the curtain.

'Miriam, where's Miriam?' cried Mrs Waters suddenly.

'I'm right here, Mother. There's no need to worry. It's just like in the old days, you at the piano . . .' she turned her head, as though noticing Gracie for the first time.

'Ladies and Gentlemen, Boys and Girls,' Gracie called again, louder. 'Please return to your seats.'

'Mama, how about my favourite Christmas song . . .'

Mrs Waters nodded and lifted the piano lid. Her fingers moved swiftly and assuredly over the keys.

Miriam joined Gracie at the microphone. 'Tell them I will sing.'

That might work. Gracie cleared her throat. 'The Blackpool Tower Children's Ballet is proud to present a very special Christmas treat for you. A one-off special solo performance by your favourite singer – Blackpool's Little Miri . . .'

'*The first noël, the angels did say . . .*' her voice as luscious as velvet.

The audience began to join in, '*was to certain poor shepherds in fields as they lay . . .*'

Now Gracie had to find George. She dashed up the stage steps and ducked behind the red velvet drape, as Mr Linnet had done.

The dancers were crying and wailing at the back of the stage. Gracie frantically scanned them all for her brother.

Madame Petrova was standing under the swaying aeroplane,

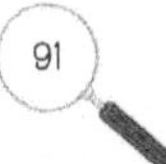

her face as white as the faux snow. '*Pozhaluysta*, do not move,' she cried.

Natalya was rigid in the cockpit, her teeth gritted, as the aeroplane lurched to one side.

'Pa! She's going to fall to her death,' cried Ruth. 'Help!'

'Where's Chadwick?' he called.

'Here!' the caretaker called, entering from the eaves with a huge step ladder.

He positioned it under the rigging and clambered up the steps. 'It's holding for now, but the winch has jammed.'

'Can you fix it?' asked Mr Linnet.

'Not without my toolbox. Goodness knows where it's gone,' he grumbled under his breath. 'Don't worry, Madame, Harry and me will get her down.'

'Get those girls out of here,' called Mr Linnet.

'I want everyone to return to the dressing rooms,' called Frances, her tone that of a formidable headmistress. 'Ruth, take the youngest ones and give them some sweet milk to settle their nerves. The rest of you girls, stop acting like drama queens and line up sensibly – the last thing we need is another accident.'

Now where was George? Gracie bit her lip. He hadn't come down into the audience. She had to hope he was safe backstage.

* * *

The backstage corridor was a total contrast to the ballroom. The wallpaper was peeling and broken chairs had been left abandoned. Gracie could feel her shoes sticking to the worn away floor.

'I'm coming for you, George!' she called.

Something moved in the shadows.

'Gracie!'

He must be close.

'Stay where you are,' she called back. 'Wait for me, George.'

Strange laughter echoed in the distance. Someone was running the other way – no, two people.

Was he with one of the dancers? Was whoever had tampered with the aeroplane hiding here? She gasped – did they have George?

She began to run. Her breathing seemed extra loud. She stumbled over a forgotten mop, passed a row of lockers, a large wire cage containing stained tablecloths and a few torn chair cushions.

She paused to catch her breath.

There was a muffled sobbing sound. It seemed to be coming from the wire cage.

Gracie leant in. There was a loud sniff.

'George?' She peeled off the top tablecloth and ruffled his hair. 'Come out of there. You're in enough trouble as it is . . . What on earth were you doing on stage?'

'Shush,' he glanced nervously from side to side, his eyes were red and puffy, 'they'll hear you.'

'Who will?' Gracie scratched her head. 'The other dancers aren't here. Luckily for you, I don't think they realised you were a boy.'

'I'm not hiding from the girls . . .'

There was a clattering at the end of the corridor.

Gracie's stomach swirled. 'Who's there?'

'His helpers . . .' then he gasped and clammed his lips tight.

'Come on, tell me,' said Gracie, stroking his arm.

He shook his head and wriggled further into the laundry. 'I promised.'

'Promised *who*?'

George began to cry.

'Hey, it's all right.' She was making him more scared, she needed to find another way to get him to open up. 'I know, let's play charades. That way you aren't really breaking your promise!'

George thought about it, then nodded. He pushed up out of the tablecloths and clambered from the wire cage.

He stood in front of her, blinking nervously.

She held up a finger. Then turned her hand upside down and made two fingers walk. Trying to suggest, *one person?*

He shook his head and held up two fingers. Then mimicked the sign for running.

She copied him; her forehead wrinkled with confusion.

George held up two fingers and twisted his hand on to its side then lowered it.

So, they were small; children not grown-ups. Could it be two of the dancers?

Gracie held up two fingers, pointed at her eyes and then indicated between herself and George for children?

He placed his hands over his eyes.

So, he hadn't seen them.

George tapped the side of his head, remembering something. He tugged at his clothing.

He stuck his nose in the air and paraded up and down like someone important. He ran his hands over his arms and torso.

Gracie rested her chin on her hand.

George looked at her expectedly.

She shook her head.

He dropped to his knees and crawled about on four legs, snarling silently. Then jumped up and pretended to be the VIP again, stroking himself once more.

An answer pinged into her head. 'They wore fur coats!'

George nodded. He brushed past Gracie, to show what had happened.

Then he leaned in and whispered. 'I heard them laughing, Gracie. They were laughing at what had happened to Natalya.'

Anger filled Gracie's chest and she thumped down hard on the laundry. 'We've got to go after them.'

'I don't want to. I want to stay here.'

'Don't be silly, we're going together. Like Sherlock Holmes

and Dr Watson!' Gracie led him down the dark corridor, slowly following its twists and turns. Eventually they reached a set of stairs, and they made their way down them.

A strange shrieking sound rang out.

George clutched Gracie's arm. 'I'm scared.'

'We've got to keep going.' She breathed in deeply. What would she do when she caught up with the saboteurs? Would she have to fight? How would she stop them from getting away?

The floor had begun to slope. They were somewhere in the depths of the Tower.

The corridor was coming to an end. She slowed and held out her arm to keep her brother at bay. *Miriam Waters wears a fur coat. Could it be her?* 'Get behind me,' she urged in a hushed tone.

Gracie stepped forward on to a tiled floor. There was a smell of hay and a horsey mustiness. They were in a stable. Six beautiful dappled grey horses whinnied as they passed their stalls.

'We must be under the circus ring,' she said. 'This must be where they keep all the animal acts.' Her throat tightened as she pictured lions and tigers close by. She hoped they were chained up. Her brother's frantic breath was hot on the back of her neck.

More laughter ricocheted off the walls making the hairs on her arms stand on end. George was right, it did sound like there were at least two of them.

They carried on, coming to a door marked PROPS.

She slowed, suddenly unsure of her pursuit. Should she go back? Find a grown-up?

'Wait there,' said Gracie, easing the door open.

The room was unlit. She crept forward, her heart hammering in her chest. What was she doing?

'Ow!' Something soft whacked against her left arm and bounced on to the floor.

There was a shrieking sound.

Gracie stepped back, changing her mind about going in, but she slipped on something and fell back. She tried to get up, instinctively reaching out. 'George, help me.'

Someone took her hand and pulled. She felt their fur coat against her skin.

The ceiling light suddenly snapped on.

'You!' cried Gracie. 'I should have known.'

Chapter Twelve
Behind Bars

'Molly and Mandy!' Gracie wagged a finger at the chimpanzees. 'So, it's *you two* that have been stealing the ballet shoes.' The apes had made a pile of the pale pink pumps in the middle of the room.

George gave a relieved laugh. 'I thought they were evil elves!' He stepped away from the light switch and picked up the ballet shoe that they'd thrown. 'They've got dozens of them!'

Gracie picked up the one she'd tripped over.

'We've been on a wild chimp chase,' said Gracie. 'I thought we'd found the saboteur, but chimps can't send threatening letters or scupper aeroplane props.'

The chimps began to chatter and started tugging at

George's tutu. 'They want my costume! Mandy and Molly want to be in the Children's Ballet,' he said, laughing.

'Mandy and Molly like pretty clothing,' said Gracie, remembering the frilly pink and blue dresses they'd worn in the café. Now they were as nature intended! She giggled, remembering how George had thought their thick black hair was a fur coat. 'It seems Molly and Mandy are as good with locks as they are knots. They've been breaking out of the menagerie and having all kinds of fun.' She wagged a finger at them. 'Well, the games up, girls, as you would say, George. We're confiscating all these ballet slippers!'

The chimps bared their teeth and started throwing the pumps in the air.

'That's enough!' shouted Gracie.

Mandy and Molly stuck out their tongues and picked up an armful of ballet shoes and pelted them at Gracie.

'Ow!' cried Gracie. 'Stop that! Help me, George.'

George dropped his tutu, revealing a pair of shorts. He stuck his hand in his pocket and pulled out a half-eaten bar of chocolate. He waved it at the apes. He nibbled at the edge. 'It's so delicious.'

The chimpanzees let go of the last ballet shoes and began jumping up and down, clapping their hands above their head.

'You'd like some, wouldn't you?' teased George, as Molly and Mandy crept closer, reaching out for the chocolate.

'Well done, George. Now we need to lead them back to the menagerie,' said Gracie. 'We'll come back later and return these to the dancers.'

'Come on, Molly and Mandy,' said George.

'I still don't understand what you are doing here, George,' said Gracie. 'Where's Phyllis?'

George scrunched up his nose. 'I swapped places with her.'

'You did what!'

'I wanted to be the spy, but you never even considered me. So, I told Phyllis you didn't need her any more. Then I borrowed her costume and ballet shoes.'

'George! Does Ma know you're here?'

'I told her I was going out to play – only I got the tram to The Tower instead. I'm not a little kid any more.'

'You're still only ten.' She shook her head. 'I'll have to ring her from *The Gazette*.'

* * *

The Blackpool Tower Menagerie was hot and smelly. Gracie's nose twitched at the mixture of straw bedding, food and dung. The air was filled with the sound of birdsong, coming from the aviary at the far end.

The room bustled with families; children running from cage to cage, calling 'come and see'. She scanned the room for Hilda or Mr Ramsbottom. How would they get to the chimp's cage without being mobbed?

The enclosures looked much too small for the animals, and the metal bars were prison like. Labels above each cage named the species inside, lion, lioness, bear . . .

A little girl and her mother were laughing at Wallace, a male lion, who strolled up and down his cage making a sound like a steam train. '*Chuff, chuff, chuff.*'

'Let's carry the chimps,' said Gracie, opening her arms for Mandy. 'It will be like having a cuddle.'

George smiled at her and picked up Molly.

They walked past a long plinth, topped with benches, until they reached the chimps' cage.

It was unlike the others; it was dressed in bunting and set out with a table and two chairs. On the table were two sets of plates, teacups and saucers and a little brass bell in the centre.

Hilda, the zoo keeper, was sitting on one of two small chairs, her head in her hands.

'Lost someone?' asked Gracie.

Hilda looked up – then grinned. 'Wherever did you find them?' She stood up so Molly and Mandy could take their places.

'Under the Tower Circus,' Gracie replied. There was no need to tell Hilda they'd been stealing ballet shoes too. The chimps were in enough trouble.

'This isn't the first time they've got out! I don't know how

they're doing it. Mr Ramsbottom completely lost his rag with me when he saw they'd gone!'

'Do lots of animals escape?' asked George gleefully.

'No, thank goodness. Well, there was that time the python got out from the snake pit.'

'Snake pit!' said George. 'Can we see it?'

'Sorry, pal,' said Hilda. 'It's not there any more. It was part of The Around the World exhibit in the Tower roof gardens – a showcase of music, dance and art from Africa, Asia and South America. There were demonstrations on costume and traditional storytelling, it was wonderful. And then there was the snake pit, you could walk right over it, and the snake handlers would bring all these different types up close to visitors; harmless grass snakes, poisonous cobras and three-foot-long pythons.'

'What happened?' asked George, eyes wide.

'Well, it was a hot day and one of the pythons had been particularly bad tempered as it was shedding its skin. Somehow, this huge python had got out and no one could find it! It was pandemonium! People were jammed on the stairs, all trying to get out at once.'

Gracie shuddered, imagining being crushed in a panicking crowd. 'Well, at least the chimps are safely back.' She smiled as they played with the teacups.

'I'll have to put new locks on their cage,' said Hilda, rubbing her brow. 'I owe you another big thank you. Sorry I didn't have time to say so properly in the Oriental Lounge yesterday. Mr Ramsbottom doesn't like me chatting on duty.'

'Mr Sheep's bum,' sniggered George.

'He is an' all,' said Hilda. 'He's horrid.'

Young children began to gather around the cage, peering in through the bars. Molly picked up the bell and it made a tinkling sound.

'You little imps! I've a good mind to cancel your tea party.' Hilda picked up a large metal teapot and a milk jug. 'Ladies . . .'

The chimps picked up their teacup and held it out so it could be filled.

The children began to giggle and clap.

Hilda tipped the milk jug first, then she poured a stream of what looked more like water than tea into their cups.

The chimps cupped their tea and drank enthusiastically.

Next Hilda gave Molly and Mandy a plate of brightly coloured jam tarts. The chimps stretched out their long hairy fingers and sniffed the tarts suspiciously, before stuffing the sweet pastries into their mouths.

Finally, Hilda presented them with a dish of fruit. The two chimps each pulled out a banana and ate it.

The crowd applauded and drifted away.

'They are very clever,' said Gracie.

'Too clever, if you ask me!' replied Hilda. 'They do learn quick. Mr Ramsbottom is always teaching them new tricks.'

She cleared the table. 'Still, he gives them nice rewards. On hot days they get orange juice ice lollies! I tell you; these animals eat better than me! I've only got sardine paste sandwiches.'

'They seem happy,' said Gracie.

'Can we see the elephants next?' asked George.

'The elephants belong to the circus, not the menagerie,' replied Hilda. 'You might see them on the beach in the mornings though, when their trainers take them for a stroll and a bathe in the sea!'

'I'd love a pet elephant.' George guffawed. 'But we'd have to get a bigger toilet put in. Imagine how much poo they do!'

'About 300lbs a day,' said Hilda, locking the chimps' cage door.

'Can we see some more animals?' asked George.

'Of course!' Hilda pointed up to an enclosure. 'That's Tilly, our ring-tailed lemur. She decided she wanted to pay her neighbours a visit.'

George giggled. 'What happened?'

'Well, she got into the cage below hers.'

'Oh no!' said Gracie wincing. The cage contained three porcupines with sharp quills.

'Luckily, we managed to snatch her to safety just as Felix, Diana and Ginger were returning home!'

'What a funny story – would you mind if I write it up for *The Gazette*?'

Hilda shrugged. 'Not at all, we are always looking for publicity – and it has a happy ending. Now, you'll want to see the jubilee cubs, of course . . .'

Gracie grinned at George. 'Yes, please.'

The cubs were four Bengal tigers. 'We were surprised they all survived,' said Hilda. 'They're six months old now and doing well. They, and mum Ranée, get a couple of pounds of goat meat and veal every day!'

'Where's their pa?' asked George.

They both missed their pa, but he had a new family now and they rarely heard from him.

'Is that him?' Gracie pointed three cages down.

'That's right. Rajah was captured in the wild a couple of years ago. Proper feisty, he is!'

'Hilda! What have I told you about chatting with friends while on duty?' called Mr Ramsbottom, suddenly appearing from behind a potted palm. He was pushing a wheelbarrow filled with old newspapers and straw. 'The aviaries all need relining with paper and the bedding needs replacing in the monkey's cages.' He jangled his keys impatiently. 'I've got to go down to the aquarium. Get on with it, girl.'

'All right. Keep your hair on,' mumbled Hilda.

George sniggered.

'WHAT did you say?'

'Nothing, Mr Ramsbottom.'

'We'd best be going any road,' said Gracie.

She and George left the menagerie and headed back downstairs. 'Come on, let's collect those ballet shoes.'

Chapter Thirteen

Another Letter

Gracie could hear chatter from the other side of the dancers' changing-room door. George readjusted his grip on the wastepaper bin full of ballet shoes.

She knocked then and popped her head round the door. Ruth and Frances were sitting together. Ruth's face was streaked from tears. 'Can my brother and I come in? We've something to show you.'

'What?' asked Ruth, wiping her face.

'Your ballet shoes,' said George, following Gracie. 'The chimps pinched them.' He placed the bin on the floor.

'Yes, Molly and Mandy from the menagerie have been getting out. It seems they've taken a liking to your ballet shoes and have been collecting them under the circus ring. I thought you'd want to know it has nothing to do with the poison pen letter.'

'We don't care about missing ballet shoes,' said Frances, standing. 'You seem to think this is some silly game,' she said, pointing at George. 'I saw you flouncing about on stage.'

'I wasn't flouncing, I was investigating,' said George, folding his arms, defiantly.'

It's OK, George. The girls are upset,' said Gracie.

'Of course we are!' said Frances. 'Natalya is lucky to be alive. We *all* are. If that plane had fallen!' She shuddered. 'Natalya's been taken to hospital – Madame thinks it's some kind of a breakdown.'

'There's been another letter an' all,' said Ruth. She passed a pale blue envelope to Gracie. PETROVA was written on the front in the same stencil-like lettering.

Gracie studied it carefully. 'No fingerprints this time.' There was no stamp again, and the stationery was the same British Bulldog brand. 'Where did you find it?'

'It was pushed under Natalya's dressing-room door.'

Gracie pulled out the paper. The message was in the same cut-out headline letters.

THIS IS YOUR FINAL WARNING

YoU ARE nOt WANTED hERE LEAVE oR YOU WILL REGRET IT

There was a knock on the door.

'Who is that?' asked Ruth, jumping.

Frances got up to find out.

It was a man in a suit. He didn't speak, just thrust a letter into the dancer's hand and turned on his heels.

She tore open the envelope and read the contents.

Frances groaned. 'They've cancelled the rest of the run.' She passed the letter to Gracie. 'They didn't even have the nerve to tell us in person.'

Gracie read it aloud. *'Blackpool Tower Management has made the difficult decision to terminate this year's Children's Ballet production with immediate effect. The Tower will instead offer additional Fredini concerts tonight (Friday,) Saturday 21st Dec (matinee and evening) and Monday 23rd Dec (evening). The Management will advertise for a new Children's Ballet director in the New Year. We thank Madame Petrova for her efforts.*

'But that's not fair,' said Gracie.

'I could have taken over for Natalya,' said Frances quietly.

'The show must go on,' agreed Ruth.

'You have to tell the Management that someone is trying to force you out. They have to reconsider this decision.'

* * *

George had talked non-stop all the way to *The Gazette* offices; all about the chimps and how awful his costume had been.

Gracie had gone straight to Mr Grime's office to tell him about the accident. He'd been concerned for Gracie and George, first of all, immediately ringing their Ma. Then he'd ordered one of the senior reporters over to the Tower. She'd been surprised when he'd asked if she felt up to writing an account too, and she'd been even more surprised that she felt excited at the challenge.

'There you go, sweetheart,' said Rosie, the tea lady, as she placed a mug of tea and a piece of fruit cake in front of George.

'That'll keep you quiet while your sister finishes typing up her story,' added Ava.

At least George seemed in much better spirits, perhaps she could quiz him some more. 'Isn't it funny how you thought Molly and Mandy were two children and a grown up . . .'

He began to pluck the raisins from his cake, discarding them on his plate. 'I told you, I had my eyes shut.'

'You didn't even take a peep?'

He shook his head, fervently.

'But you saw everything that happened before the accident

. . .' led Gracie. 'Did you see anyone acting suspiciously?' She was remembering now how Mr Linnet had been late to his seat. 'Did you see the pianist, Harry Linnet?'

He clamped his lips tight and shook his head.

Gracie wrinkled her nose. 'What about a man in a boiler suit – Neville Chadwick? He might have been looking for his toolbox.'

George scowled and shook his head harder.

'What about an old lady? Mrs Waters? She might have been wandering around backstage too. Did you see her near the plane?'

He gritted his teeth. 'No.'

'You definitely didn't see anyone else? Someone near the plane?'

George's cheeks burned. 'I told you. No.'

'Ho, ho, ho!' bellowed Mr Grime, striding out from his office into the newsroom dressed as Father Christmas!

Gracie grinned at George, but he was suddenly spluttering, his face as white as a Majestic bed sheet.

She quickly patted him on the back. 'Don't eat so fast,' she scolded.

The newsroom staff were applauding.

'You look a bit skinny for Father Christmas,' called Dennis. 'You want a pillow under that red jacket.'

Mr Grime adjusted the thick black belt at his waist. 'Will I do, though? I don't want the kiddies to realise I'm a stand-in for the real Father Christmas.'

'You look great,' said Rosie. 'There's not many Father Christmas's with a real beard!'

'Thank you,' Mr Grime grinned, then turned to George. 'And what would you like as a present, young man?' He leaned closer. 'Have you been good for Father Christmas?'

George jumped up. 'I need the toilet.'

Gracie sighed. 'They're down that corridor.'

George sprinted off towards the toilets.

'Now, Father Christmas is looking for some good boys and girls to help out at the Tower's Christmas Eve Children's Party,' continued the editor.

There was a loud groan, followed by laughter.

'I need a volunteer to be my assistant.' He held up a green outfit. 'Who would like to be my elf?'

Around the room the staff began to mutter excuses.

'There must be someone . . .'

'I'll do it,' said Gracie. This was her chance to get back into the Tower. She couldn't believe her luck.

'Well done, Gracie, what a fine example you set. There'll be an extra Christmas bonus for you.'

The room *awwed* with envy.

He handed her a costume. Gracie noticed the Jokes Galore label on it as she put it in her bag.

'*Gazette!*' called a young lad with curly hair who had entered the newsroom pushing a trolley. He offered out the first papers, hot off the press. The reporters and subs flicked through checking everything was in order.

Gracie took her copy with a shaky hand. The ink was still a bit damp and left black marks on her fingertips as she turned the pages to find her article about popular Christmas toys. Her by-line was at the top of the first paragraph. She grinned with pride.

She hurried down the corridor to the toilets and knocked on the door.

'George! Are you in there?' she called.

The door swung open.

'George! Have you been crying?'

'I want to go home. I'm tired.'

'I'm sorry, George. I know you are. Ma will be here soon, I'm sure.'

'I don't want to go back in there.' He stood tight to the wall. 'I don't like it.'

'OK, why don't you sit in reception and look through the paper, see my name's on it!'

He pushed the paper away. 'I want to wait outside for Ma,' said George, pulling her towards the front of the building.

'Fine!' snapped Gracie. 'I don't know why I let you come here anyway. Acting like a baby! Go and wait for Ma. I've got work to do.'

* * *

Mr Grime passed Gracie's typed up story back to her. 'Well, Miss Fairshaw, it looks like you've got your first front page splash! Congratulations.'

Mr Grime pulled out a rectangular card, small enough to fit into a wallet. Then he picked up his fountain pen and began to write on it. 'This is a press card.'

There was a head and shoulders photograph of herself on one side. A wave of excitement flooded through her.

PRESS

THIS WILL IDENTIFY

Gracie Fairshaw

***Blackpool Gazette* Journalist**

'You can show it to prove you're a journalist,' explained Mr Grime. 'It comes with certain rights and responsibilities. You may get asked to show it at a crime scene by the police, by a clerk at the Magistrate's Court or to get into a council meeting.'

Mr Grime passed the card to her. Gracie felt as though he was also passing an unspoken expectation on to her. This card opened up new powers to her, and she would take great care of it.

'You need to sign it,' said Mr Grime, offering her the fountain pen.

Gracie signed her name on the dotted line. She felt so grown up!

'We'll see you in the morning then. Just a half day shift on a Saturday.'

Chapter Fourteen
The Archive

Gracie had slept barely a wink, her mind going over and over the events of the last few days, but she wasn't the only one who'd had a troubled night.

George pushed away his porridge. 'I'm not hungry.'

'Not hungry?' asked Ma. 'You're never not hungry! You're not sickening, are you? I've heard there's a bug going around.' She clamped her palm to his forehead. 'Hmm, you don't *feel* hot. When did you last go to the toilet? Perhaps I should give you some syrup of figs to get things moving.'

'Ugh, no, I'm not ill,' moaned George. 'I'm just not hungry.'

'But Ma's right, you're never not hungry,' said Gracie.

'Well, I am today, so just LEAVE ME ALONE.'

'George! Apologise for speaking to me like that!'

He mumbled sorry.

'Now tell me what's the matter.' Ma narrowed her eyes. 'Have you done something to put yourself on Father Christmas's naughty list? It's best you tell me.'

'I haven't done nuthin'.'

'Come on, it can't be that bad. Have you broken something? Lost something?'

'I haven't, 'onest.'

'If you don't tell me, Father Christmas won't come.'

'I don't care!' He ran from the room.

'Oh dear. I hope he isn't coming down with something,' said Ma.

'I heard him calling out in the night,' said Gracie. 'I think he was having a bad dream.' Chasing the chimps down that corridor must still be playing on his mind.

'I think you might be right,' said Ma. 'I found his letter to Father Christmas in his room.' She handed a crumpled piece of paper to Gracie. 'I bet he's having nightmares about wild animals.'

Gracie read the letter.

Dear Father Christmas,

Please can I have a bear or a lion or an elefant for Christmas insted of a cannun. A baby one would be pearfect as I've not sorted out acomodayshun yet. I have been quite good this year.

George Fairshaw, 10,
The Majestic
Blackpool.

Gracie laughed. 'Oh, Ma! How on earth will Father Christmas pull that off!'

'I have no idea – and as if we haven't got enough pets in the house! Imagine having a wild beast move in!' She shook her head. 'I suppose I could take him to the new toy department at R.H.O. Hills to pick something more reasonable!'

'Let me take him,' said Gracie. 'He could meet me in town at three.'

'I'm not sure I want him getting the tram on his own again,' said Ma. 'What was he thinking!'

'Well, he is ten, as he keeps reminding us.'

'I still think of him as my little boy. I suppose I have to let George have a bit more freedom now he's growing up. Hopefully some fresh air will make him feel better, but I'll give him some malt syrup and make sure he has a nap first, to be sure.'

'We could call on Audrey Mosson afterwards; I've meaning to see how she's feeling,' said Gracie. 'I'll give her a ring.'

* * *

'Good morning,' said Ava, as Gracie took off her coat and sat at her desk. 'I've a pile of press releases here that need rewriting, see if there's a local angle, and if there is, get some fresh quotes.'

'Oh, yes, of course.' She hadn't expected more stories to work on so soon, and so many!

'Don't worry, most of these will only make NIBs,' said Ava, smiling.

'A *what*?' A nib was the end of a pencil, wasn't it?

'A news-in-brief, snippets, grout, the small filler articles you see in the columns on the edge of a page. Why press officers think we'll want three pages on a new widget is beyond me. But be careful, there's always a slim chance one of these press releases might make a good lead story. If you're not sure, ask me.'

There were a lot of journalism terms to remember. *It's like a whole new language,* thought Gracie.

She worked hard on the press releases for the next couple of hours. Ava was right, they weren't particularly interesting, but it still felt very satisfying crossing through each one then thrusting them down on to her spike.

'Ava, how can I find out where someone lives?' asked Gracie.

'Well, if they are over the age of twenty-one and registered to vote you can try *The Gazette*'s copy of the electoral register. Want me to show you where it's kept?'

'Yes, please.'

She followed Ava to the back of the newsroom.

'Welcome to the archive,' she opened the door.

The room was lined with shelves bearing large, heavy-

looking ledgers. Against the walls were two desks and six large filing cabinets.

'If you need to do research, this is the place to come,' explained Ava. 'It's a real treasure house.'

'I don't see any crowns or jewels,' joked Gracie.

'Ha, you're right, but it is full of golden nuggets when you're trying to research a back story or track down a potential source.'

'Sauce?'

'With an *ou*. A journalist's source is someone who gives you information, sometimes off the record.'

'Now I'm even more confused,' said Gracie.

'It just means they want to be anonymous, and that you can't say who told you.'

'I see.'

Gracie peered at the large ledgers. The labels all said BACK ISSUES, with dates going as far back as 1873.

'You'll find past copies of *The Gazette* in those,' explained Ava. 'There's a cuttings file an' all. It's where we keep articles from rival local papers and the Nationals – that's newspapers which are published across the country. They can be handy for writing background.'

Ava pulled open one of the metal cabinets. 'This is where we store photographs.' She pulled out a black-and-white image of the Tower. 'Some of these are used again and again.

'These shelves are where you'll find local maps, reference

books, spare telephone directories and, ah, here you go, the Blackpool electoral register.' Ava placed it on the table. 'Shout me if you need further assistance.'

'I will.' Gracie sat down and opened the electoral register. She folded the pages back. The listings were in a small print and broken up into electoral wards, and then ordered alphabetically by surname, first names and place of abode. It was going to take some time to search through.

Her eyes felt like the words were swimming in front of her.

Streets, avenues, closes, ways, drives, crescents, roads – she hadn't realised there were so many different types.

Then there were the wards – Alexandra, Bispham, Brunswick, Foxhall, Layton, Marton, Stanley, Tyldesley, Victoria . . .

At last, she found it.

Waters, Nora. Lindale Gardens – and listed at the same address, *Waters, Miriam.* The ex-ballet director lived near the greyhound stadium. Gracie didn't know that area of Blackpool very well, even though it wasn't too far from The Majestic. She could call on Saturday morning. She had to double check that the trouble at the ballet had coincided with Madame Petrova's appointment as director. 'Was Mrs Waters really happy to retire? And did the former director know Mr Chadwick is carrying a torch for her?'

Gracie wrote the address down in her notebook and put the file back on the shelf. Now she opened the metal cabinet containing old photographs.

She flicked carefully through the paper folders inside. Each was labelled with a tag containing a description of the contents. There were folders for councillors, local theatre stars, stock photographs of important buildings and, finally, a folder marked Blackpool Tower.

Gracie eased the folder up so she could investigate the contents. There were photographs of the tower being constructed and completed. She moved on to the interior shots – circus, aquarium, ballroom, menagerie. There was a separate large manilla envelope for the Children's Ballet.

She emptied the contents on to one of the desks. There were line ups of entire casts going back years – photographs of Mrs Waters with Little Miri as a child, and finally a more recent picture taken in the summer at Mrs Waters's retirement party. Miriam had her arms around her adopted mother's waist, with Audrey, Frances and Ruth looking on.

She turned to a large file containing back copies of *The Gazette*. She found the same photo in one of the July editions. It was the main piece on page three.

TOWER BALLET DIRECTOR'S FINAL BOW

Dancers past and present gathered in the Blackpool Tower Ballroom on Saturday to congratulate Mrs Nora Waters on her retirement.

Mrs Waters has overseen the Blackpool Tower Children's Ballet for thirty years, producing and directing dozens of spectacular Christmas shows.

Gracie scanned the rest of the article. It was a straightforward summary of Mrs Waters's career. There was a long list of people present at the party and a description of several gifts presented to Mrs Waters, including a carriage clock and a copy of a Degas painting.

'Wait, this is interesting,' Gracie said.

Blackpool Tower's Management have confirmed that they are in discussions with Miriam 'Little Miri' Waters, Mrs Waters's protégé and adopted daughter, regarding the future of the ballet.

Ms Waters, the ballet's most successful ballerina, refused to confirm or deny that she has agreed to take over as Director and Producer.

'Tonight is about the past, not the future,' said Ms Waters. 'We are here to celebrate the ballet's wonderful achievements under my mother's leadership.'

'Miriam Waters was in line for Madame Petrova's job! That gives her a big motive for sabotaging the ballet!' She closed the file. *I'll have to question Little Miri too! She would know her way around backstage.*

She would question them both, but there was someone else she wanted to speak to first.

Chapter Fifteen

Off the Record

Gracie had her press pass ready again, should anyone stop her, but she'd not needed it once she was past the concierge at the Tower's entrance.

She leant on a cast iron radiator and warmed herself for a moment before knocking on the door marked CARETAKER.

When there was no answer, she turned the handle and snuck inside, her heart racing.

The walls were lined with carpentry tools of varying sizes, all carefully labelled. Hammers, saws, screwdrivers, wood chisels and files. Gracie wrinkled her nose at the strong smell of varnish, turps and sawdust.

She was surprised to see Neville Chadwick sitting at a large work desk, facing the wall. He was focused on a wooden box he was polishing with beeswax. He hadn't heard her knock as he was listening to a boxing match on a wireless.

Gracie coughed.

He still didn't hear. She coughed louder.

She reached out and touched his shoulder.

Neville jumped out of his chair and twisted round. 'You nearly gave me a heart attack,' he growled, quickly grabbing the box and shoving it into the desk drawer under some red felt. 'Who are you?' He quickly put on the glasses that were resting on top of his head. 'What do you want?'

Gracie held out her press pass. 'I'm working for *The Gazette*.'

He jumped to his feet. 'A reporter!' His cheeks were puffed up like a bull seal. 'Why, you sneak!'

She staggered back. He was a big man and as he towered over her, Gracie felt truly afraid.

'I don't speak to reporters! Get out!' he cried, thrusting the metal file dangerously close to her face.

'Put the file down, please, Mr Chadwick,' pleaded Gracie, her voice trembling, 'before one of us gets hurt.'

'You heard the girl,' said Mr Linnet, suddenly entering the room.

Neville Chadwick looked down at the file, as though he had only just realised it was in his grasp.

'She shouldn't be in here,' he opened his hand and let the tool clatter on to his desk.

'Well, you can't blame the girl for trying to get an interview with the hero of the moment, Neville,' said Mr Linnet.

The caretaker blinked. 'What are you talking about?'

'The way you stayed calm and got Natalya down. All the Tower staff are saying you deserve a medal. You can understand the papers wanting to praise you too.'

Gracie spied a chance to make her case. 'We want to run an editorial – we think the council should formally acknowledge your bravery. You *and* Mr Linnet, of course – he helped too, didn't he?'

Chadwick narrowed his eyes and huffed at her, but he was listening, and his face was less angry.

'I was there,' said Gracie, as she tried to read his expression. 'All those girls stood underneath that swaying aeroplane, stricken with fear – but not you, Mr Chadwick, you knew exactly what to do.'

She studied the caretaker. He was a man who cared about his appearance. His shoes and belt buckle were highly polished. His cuffs and collar were brilliant white and pressed to perfection. His hair Brylcreemed smooth, not a strand out of place. He wore his overalls as though they were a uniform.

'You would know all about staying calm in the face of danger,' said Gracie. 'Men like you and my pa faced danger daily during the war.'

Chadwick's whole body softened. 'I don't want a medal

and I don't want any fuss in the paper either. If you have to put summat in, then write about Mr Linnet. He's a good man – tell your readers what a talented songwriter he is; he could do with a break. He has more talent in his little finger than that Fredini.'

'Can I quote you on that?' asked Gracie with a grin.

His face twitched, almost letting a smile form. 'You're a cheeky one.'

'Well, if we're all friends, I'll be off,' said Mr Linnet. 'I only popped by to tell you there's still no sign of it.'

'I knew it, someone's swiped it. I told you,' said Mr Chadwick. 'All me best tools, pinched.'

Mr Linnet shrugged his shoulders, before retreating. 'You can try telling the Management, but I think they've got bigger concerns at the moment.'

Mr Chadwick grunted. 'They'll cost me a fortune to replace.'

Gracie scratched her nose. Mr Chadwick could have loosened the scenery and tampered with the aeroplane, but he was also most likely to be blamed. Now it looked like the saboteur had stolen some tools. Had Mr Linnet really looked everywhere? Could he have taken the tools?

She would have to think about it more later. Time was ticking on. 'Would you speak off the record?' Gracie chanced.

'About the accident?' his eyebrows lowered.

'I just want some background information. Have you worked at the Tower a long time?'

'Mrs Waters hired me herself in 1920,' he said proudly.

'Do you make the sets?' asked Gracie.

'No, no. I only do repairs – there's a whole team involved in construction, then the stagehands put it all in place.'

'And each year's show has a different theme?'

'Well, usually, but this year Madame Petrova decided to recycle some of the old scenery. There was quite a panic when some pieces were accidentally thrown away.'

'So, Madame Petrova had nothing to do with the planning for this year's show?'

He shook his head, 'Mrs Waters always started work on the new Christmas show each January. Madame Petrova only had a few weeks and she had to go along with Mrs Waters's original idea. That's why it's all been a bit last minute, calling in favours to find some extra set dressing.'

'What about the aeroplane, was that old?'

Mr Chadwick was angry again. 'It was in perfect order when I installed it. The plane should never have dropped like that. The winch was fine when I did the final checks.'

Could she believe him or had Neville Chadwick been lying from the start? He could have thrown away the scenery himself as an alibi and then damaged the replacement. He certainly had the skills to damage the aeroplane; had he calculated that putting himself in the frame would make others quickly dismiss his guilt?

But if he was telling the truth, he might be a witness. 'Have you seen anyone suspicious hanging around?' Gracie asked.

'There haven't been any strangers, if that's what you mean,' said Mr Chadwick. 'The stage door is manned at all times, especially after the problem with the scenery. The only people allowed backstage, other than me, are the crew and performers. I saw Natalya there in her Father Christmas outfit, and that's it.'

Chapter Sixteen

Mrs Waters' Secret

Gracie felt nervous as she walked up the path to the Waters' front door. She knew if she was going to be a successful reporter she would have to get used to knocking on strangers' doors and asking them questions.

The path was lined with empty flowerpots and the paint on the window boxes was flaking. The former ballet director seemed to have lost interest in her garden.

Gracie took hold of the knocker and rapped it against the wood, then she gripped her press card inside her coat pocket, unsure whether to show it or not.

After a few seconds, the door opened. 'Hello,' said Mrs Waters. 'How lovely, a visitor.'

'Hello, Mrs Waters. My name is Gracie Fairshaw. I work at

The Gazette.'

'Who is it?' called Miriam from inside the house. 'Mother, what have I told you about answering the door.'

Mrs Waters was staring at Gracie. 'Oh, I wasn't expecting anyone from *The Gazette.*' She patted her white hair. 'How lovely.'

'Yes, I've come to ask you about the Children's Ballet.'

'Oh yes,' said Mrs Waters. 'Do you want to know about my new show? It's going to be wonderful. My best yet.'

'Who are you?' asked Miriam, pushing round her mother. 'What do you want?' The younger woman had dark shadows under her eyes and her hair had been pulled back into an untidy ponytail. 'Hang on, you were at the Tower yesterday.'

'Yes. My name is Gracie Fairshaw,' she repeated. 'That's why I'm here. I'm a reporter with *The Gazette.*'

'My mother has retired,' interrupted Miriam. 'If you want to know about the Children's Ballet, you will have to speak to Madame Petrova.' She turned to Mrs Waters and said, 'Mother, come inside please, it's freezing out.'

'I think this girl is one of my dancers,' said Mrs Waters. 'Do we have an appointment, dear?'

'I'm not a dancer,' said Gracie. 'But I have come to see you, Mrs Waters.'

'How lovely to have a visitor. Come in child, we'll catch our death stood here. I'll make us a nice cup of tea, that will soon warm us up.'

'You've already got one,' said Miriam, putting a hand on her mother's arm to try and guide her in. 'I suppose you'd better come in too. You're making my mother agitated.'

Gracie felt a flush rise up her neck, but she stepped into the hallway anyway. The walls were lined with photographs, framed sheet music and old advertising posters for the Blackpool Tower Children's Ballet. Mrs Waters featured on lots of them, as did Little Miri. Gracie hadn't realised the director was as much of a local personality as her protégé and adopted daughter.

'Miriam, we'll want tea in the parlour for our guest,' said Mrs Waters, heading down the short hallway.

'The living room will be fine,' said Miriam, closing the door with a sharp bang. 'Miss Fairshaw won't be staying long.'

Before she could follow, Miriam grabbed Gracie by the shoulder.

'Ow!'

'My mother was very upset by yesterday's accident. It took me ages to get her settled last night.'

Gracie nodded. Mrs Waters was looking less and less like a suspect and more like a nice old lady who was struggling with life. She seemed more settled for the moment, fussing over the tea service and straightening the cups and saucers.

'Are you one of my pupils?' asked Mrs Waters, as she settled back into a comfy chair.

'No, I'm not,' said Gracie. 'But my friend is. Audrey Mosson.'

Mrs Waters looked confused. 'Audrey? Now, let me see. I remember Angela. Miriam, remind me, what does Audrey look like?'

'She's the Railway Queen,' said Gracie, but she hushed when Miriam glared.

'Oh, yes,' said Mrs Waters, her brow wrinkled. 'That's right.' She picked up a ginger nut from a plate, crumbs falling on to the doily. She took a bite. 'Urgh, Miriam, it tastes funny.'

Miriam held out her hand and took the biscuit. She nibbled the edge. 'It's fine, Mother,' she passed it back.

Mrs Waters took another bite, her face showing disgust, then spat it out into her hand. 'I don't like it.'

Miriam flushed, and used a napkin to gather up the partially chewed biscuit.

Gracie looked away, feeling embarrassed for both women. There was an upright piano under the window with a lovely red poinsettia on top and a framed photo of Mrs Waters and Miriam as a young girl.

'What a lovely tree,' said Gracie. The fairy lights and glass baubles were placed a bit haphazardly, as if done by a child, but the decorations were colourful and festive. 'And so many Christmas cards!' They were hanging on string in rows along the wall and propped up on every possible surface.

'They're from my girls,' said Mrs Waters proudly. 'They always send cards at Christmas. Such sweethearts.'

'There'll be cards from all the girls in this year's show,' said Gracie.

'Oh yes.' Mrs Waters added another spoonful of sugar to her tea. Was that five?

'Ruth Linnet, Harry's daughter . . .'

'Ruth?'

'That's right. She replaced Audrey in the matinee.'

Miriam gave another glare.

'Oh yes, I remember Angela,' repeated Mrs Waters. 'Very talented. I always knew she had potential.'

Gracie didn't bother correcting her again. 'Can you tell me anything about Frances Ashton?'

'What do you want to know?' asked Miriam, interrupting. 'She likes to pretend she's as tough as old boots, but she's as soft as butter underneath. Poor kid has had a tough start to life. Her temper sometimes flares up, but usually when she's defending one of the other girls. She'd do anything for them.'

'They're all good girls, especially Miriam.' Mrs Waters lowered her voice. 'Don't tell anyone, but she's my favourite. I wish she was my own daughter.'

She seems to be reliving the past, thought Gracie, *as though the present is no longer her reality.*

'Would you like to join the Children's Ballet?' Mrs Waters stirred another spoonful of sugar into her teacup. 'You know you will have to audition like all the other girls. They queue all down the promenade when we invite them to try out.'

She lifted the cup and drank, then promptly spat the tea out again. 'Oh! That's horrid!'

Miriam took the cup from her and tasted the tea. 'Urgh,' she dipped a fresh teaspoon into the sugar and dabbed it on the end of her tongue. 'It's salt! Oh Mother, you've mixed the packets up again.'

Gracie chewed her bottom lip. *That rings a bell,* she thought. *Of course – the girls said someone had put salt in the sugar bowl at the Tower!*

'I'm sorry,' said Mrs Waters. 'I'm sorry.'

'Please, Mother, it doesn't matter,' Miriam began to cry. 'I, I . . . can make anoth–' she could barely get the words out for the tears.

Gracie put her hand on Miriam's arm. 'Why don't I make you both a fresh cup.'

Miriam snivelled a thank you. 'The kitchen is across the hall.'

Gracie scanned the shelf for a tea caddy. She prised the lid off and spooned tea leaves into a silver teapot, then filled the aluminium kettle with water.

She sat the kettle on the hob and lit the gas ring. A gramophone had begun playing in the next room. Mrs Waters started to sing along.

Gracie felt a great surge of sympathy for Mrs Waters, and for

Miriam too. It was as though the mother-daughter relationship had been reversed. Now she understood the real reason that Miriam had withdrawn from accepting the role of director. All her efforts were concentrated on caring for her mother.

The kettle began to whistle, telling Gracie the water was almost ready.

She placed three clean cups on a tray, then poured the water into the teapot and let it brew.

'I thought you might need help with the tray,' said Miriam, entering the kitchen. She had the poise of a lifelong dancer and stood with a rigid back. 'You found everything then?'

'Yes, thank you,' Gracie adding a tea strainer to the tray. 'Everything is very organised.'

Miriam's eyes were bloodshot, but she had touched up her make-up. She took a deep breath. 'My mother taught me to be disciplined. All us Tower Ballet girls are. Everything we have achieved is down to her dedication. She has given the best part of her life to the company. I thought her retirement would give her a chance to focus on herself, but it hasn't turned out that way.

'I should have seen the signs that things weren't right. She would get muddled, forgetful. Stories would be repeated over and over, and I have to watch her like a hawk – I can't leave her for a minute.'

'It must be very difficult for you,' said Gracie, as she poured the tea.

'I thought the best thing to do was for me take over as director of the Tower Ballet. Mother would officially retire, but I would have her by my side. She is calmer when she's watching the girls perform.

'The Management wanted to make a big deal of the changes; they threw a party and invited the press. It was awful. I was terrified people would realise Mother was ill and her reputation would be ruined.' She lowered her voice. 'I don't think Mother understood she was stepping down. A few times, I've found she's made her way to the Tower. Luckily Mr Chadwick keeps an eye out for her. But then she started wandering in the middle of the night – still in her nightie!'

The former ballet director was struggling with her memory. What Gracie had questioned as potentially suspicious – Mrs Waters being backstage at the dress rehearsal, her going missing a short time before the plane had collapsed – the old lady had just been confused about where she was supposed to be.

Mrs Waters didn't want to take back control of the Children's Ballet, she thought she still *was* in charge.

'Is that when you told the Management they should advertise for a new director?' asked Gracie.

'Yes. My mother needs full-time care. I am very grateful to Madame Petrova for taking over at such short notice. She will ensure the continued success of the Tower Ballet.'

Not if the saboteur has their way, thought Gracie, as she

followed Miriam back into the living room with the tea.

Mrs Waters was holding the record's cardboard sleeve to her chest. 'This is my favourite of Little Miri's,' she said, putting the needle back to the start of the 78. 'It's a big hit.' She joined in again with the chorus. 'I'm dizzy for you, dizzy like a daffodil.'

'My mother loves to sing; it seems to calm her.'

'How long has your mother had problems with her memory?' asked Gracie quietly.

'It's hard to say exactly, I think she hid it well at first. At least a year.'

'And she was happy running the ballet? You never had a problem with silly tricks being played on any of the girls? Any mishaps or accidents?' asked Gracie.

Miriam sipped her tea while she considered the question. 'No. Nothing like yesterday, if that's what you're getting at. Girls will sometimes fall out and do petty things out of spite, but there was never anything serious. If you're looking for a story after yesterday's accident, you won't find it here. My mother ran an ordered, safe children's ballet.'

Gracie nodded. 'I'm sure she did. The girls speak very highly of her.' She glanced at the clock on the mantelpiece and swigged down a big mouthful of hot tea. 'I should be going.'

There was still a question mark hanging over Mr Chadwick, but she was certain neither Mrs Waters nor Miriam was the saboteur.

Chapter Seventeen
A Scoop

Church Street was heaving with shoppers carrying bags full of gifts. Gracie glanced into the shop windows as she hurried by. Pretty lights twinkled, tinsel glistened and piles of beautifully wrapped presents were carefully placed around small Christmas trees or pushed into stockings.

She hesitated at a gift shop, scouring the window for a suitable Get Well Soon gift, but it was nearly all tourist souvenirs. Blackpool crests were on everything – china ornaments, pink lustreware cups and saucers, pens, postcards and snow globes. There were even miniature Blackpool Towers for sale. She spotted some tea towels and song sheets featuring the Children's Ballet for sale, but Gracie didn't think Audrey would appreciate those right now.

She moved on to the sweet shop next door. The window was filled with shelves of glass jars. Gracie's eyes widened as she looked at the golden cinder toffee, pink sugar mice and brightly coloured peace babies, her mouth watering. She pushed open the door and went inside.

There were even more sweet jars! Liquorice allsorts, dolly mixtures, wine gums, sherbet lemons and aniseed balls.

Two small children were at the counter, waiting for their rainbow drops to be weighed out and poured into paper bags.

Gracie made her way over to the cash till. On the shelf behind were boxes of chocolate. She scanned the shelf, past the All Gold, – *ah, there they were!*

'A dessert chocolate apple please.'

The shopkeeper reached for one. 'Here you are, miss. Anything else?' He put it on the counter.

'A sherbet fountain and a quarter of rhubarb and custards, please.'

The man began to pour out the boiled sweets and they clattered on to the brass pan of the measuring scales.

Gracie opened her satchel and took out her purse to pay. Then, after taking her change, she put her shopping into the bag.

She headed back out into the street and made her way towards Lakin's.

A crowd had gathered around *Notes Music Shop* a little further along the parade. Her instinct was to edge away, she hated being packed in with lots of people, but then she heard Mr Grime's words in her head – 'Always keep your eyes peeled for a story.'

She took a deep breath and shoved her way to the front, the sound of piano music getting louder.

The display window was a blanket of fake snow and in the middle was a miniature piano. A girl with blonde ringlets played a jazzy version of 'Santa Claus is Coming to Town'. The mini piano sounded just like a full-size one and much better than the one they had at The Majestic!

'Isn't she good,' said a well-spoken woman. 'I might buy one for the girls.'

'Ooh, they'd love it,' said her friend. 'And they say the Duchess of York has purchased one just like it for the little princesses.'

'Aye, and only royalty could afford it,' said a Yorkshireman nearby. 'Twenty-four guineas indeed!'

She hadn't found a scoop after all. It was just the music shop's way of promoting their latest sale item. She wanted news stories not an advertisement piece.

The girl was coming to the end of the song – she gave a final flourish and the crowd began to applaud.

Gracie did a double take. The young pianist was Ruth from the Children's Ballet! Was she being paid to demonstrate the instrument? She couldn't be a potential customer, surely?

Gracie waved, and Ruth beckoned her inside.

'Lovely, isn't it?' said the ballet dancer, putting the lid down on the piano. 'I couldn't resist coming in and trying it out. Look at the wood finish and the chrome details.'

'It is very nice,' said Gracie. 'I'd be afraid to touch it, in case I damaged it.'

'Can you play then?' asked Ruth, surprise in her tone.

'My brother George and I can do chopsticks together, but I prefer listening to records than playing an instrument.'

'There's nothing better than live music,' said Ruth. 'I must admit, I much prefer playing to dancing.'

'You're very talented at both,' said Gracie.

'Thank you. What are you doing here, last minute shopping? They've got some more affordable items too.'

'Is that a polite way of saying cheap?'

Ruth laughed.

'Actually, I've got to be going,' said Gracie. 'I'm meeting my brother, but I was distracted by your lovely playing. We're going to look around R.H.O.'s new toy shop.'

'I love it in there! It's magical.'

Gracie smiled. 'Would you like to come too? We're going on to see Audrey afterwards, you could join us.'

'Oh, yes please! Let me just tell my father. He's in the sheet music department. Right, I won't be a minute.' Ruth hurried off into the basement of the shop.

* * *

'Gazette! Get your Gazette!' called the street vendor, waving a copy of the new edition in the air at passers-by.

'I'll take one, please.' Gracie handed over her money and unfolded the paper. Her stomach was fizzing with excitement at seeing her first front page story.

'Gosh,' said Ruth. 'That headline's a bit over the top, isn't it!'

DANCER IN TOWER PLUNGE
BY GRACIE FAIRSHAW

She was right. It sounded like Natalya had fallen to her death! Had the sub editor even read her story? 'I suppose they changed it to sell more papers. "Dancer safely rescued from aeroplane" wouldn't do that.'

She quickly scanned the first paragraph.

> *Panic broke out last night at the Blackpool Tower's Children's Ballet when a wooden aeroplane prop plunged from the ballroom ceiling over the terrified audience.*

Gracie pursed her lips. The opening paragraph had been altered too. She supposed the new version was more dramatic. She read on . . .

Natalya Petrova (15) was left dangling in the aeroplane for more than ten minutes while brave Tower employees battled to get the starlet down.

Mr Harold Linnet and Mr Neville Chadwick dropped the safety curtain before using a ladder to rescue the Russian-born ballerina.

SURPRISE REPRISE.

Miss Miriam Waters, better known as Blackpool favourite, 'Little Miri' made an unexpected return to the stage.

CONTINUES PAGE 2

Gracie turned the page.

'WINTER BELLES'
SABOTAGE MYSTERY

Blackpool Police have refused to confirm or deny if they have questioned the cast and crew in connection with a series of 'mishaps' at the Tower's Children's Ballet since the arrival of Madame Irina Petrova, the new director and producer. Mm Petrova originates from Russia and was brought in to replace Mrs Waters who retired last year.

'But that makes it sound like one of us could be the saboteur!' said Ruth. 'How can they print that?'

'Have you been questioned by the police?' asked Gracie.

'No, of course not – but they'll want to interrogate us now, won't they?'

'Yes, I think they will.' Gracie folded up the newspaper. It would be much harder to investigate once the police were involved.

They made their way down Bank Hey Street, under the shadow of the Tower. Gracie felt panicked again at all the shoppers. She hadn't realised it would be so busy. It was quite a contrast to quiet little Milltown where she used to live.

She gritted her teeth and headed for the main entrance to R.H.O.'s, where she and George had arranged to meet up.

There he was, tucked inside the doorway. She waved to him.

'Oh,' said George. 'I didn't know Ruth was coming with us.'

'We just bumped into each other in Notes,' she replied. 'You're feeling better then?'

'A bit.'

'That's good, because I've bought you a sherbet fountain.' Gracie handed over the paper tube.

George pulled out the liquorice stick that was poking out the end and sucked it. 'Delicious!'

Gracie offered round the bag of rhubarb and custard sweets.

'I've been doing some Christmas shopping too,' said George. 'I've been back to Jokes Galore.' He patted his pocket.

'Oh, George!' laughed Gracie. 'You'd better not play any more pranks on me.'

Gracie took a deep breath and strode into R.H.O. Hills. She tried to ignore the crowds of shoppers pushing and shoving, grabbing last minute gifts off shelves. Their eyes were steely with determination as they shuffled forward towards a row of tills, to expectant, smartly dressed shop assistants. It was a far cry from Lakin's. Everything was clean, bright, shiny and new.

Gracie focused on the pretty decorations hanging from the ceiling; multi-coloured garlands in sweeping boughs and grinning man-in-the-moon paper lanterns that were all the rage.

The sound of children's laughter and shouts rang in her ears as they made their way to the recently extended toys and games department. There were shelves and shelves filled with Mickey Mouse products. There were tea sets, paint sets, pinball, scrapbooks, musical instruments, kaleidoscopes, pull toys and skittles.

A girl wheeled past on a tricycle, almost running over Gracie's foot. She jumped back. 'Watch out!'

Gracie squeezed past two young kids with freckles who were in a game of tug of war over a magnetic fishing game.

'You know you can't really have a lion as a present,' she said to George. 'There must be something in here you'd like.'

He picked up a toy aeroplane. 'This is a bit like the one Natalya got stuck in.'

'You shouldn't keep thinking about that,' said Gracie.

'We need a distraction,' said Ruth. 'Look! There's the grotto.' She pointed at the far end of the shop. She hurried towards a line of wooden reindeers which marked the pathway to the grotto. The entrance was covered with red and gold tinsel.

George stuck his heels in. 'I want to stay here.'

'It will be fun,' said Gracie, hurrying after Ruth.

'I used to love sitting on Father Christmas's knee and whispering what I would like for Christmas,' said Ruth, as they joined the back of the line. 'I suppose I'm a bit old for all that now.'

'You're never too old for Christmas,' said Gracie.

The queue was buzzing with excited children.

'I remember the year I got a xylophone; I think that's when I realised how much I adore music,' said Ruth.

'It must be nice being from a musical family. Does your Ma play?'

'No, actually that's why she and Pa split up. He used to be in a band and was always touring. I suppose it's ironic that he was the one who chose to stay with me after they split.'

'My parents are divorced too,' said Gracie, as they moved up the line. 'It's hard, isn't it.'

Ruth nodded.

Gracie turned to check on George.

He wasn't there.

'Oh no, where has he gone?'

Ruth stood on tiptoe to try and see across the store.

'George!' cried Gracie, stepping out of the queue.

'He can't have gone far.'

Gracie's stomach churned as she worked her away along the aisle, dodging in and out of shoppers. 'George! Where are you?'

There were too many people. Their faces lunging in and out as they reached to take things from displays and shelves all around her.

She felt sick. What would Ma say if she couldn't find him?

'Do you think he's gone outside again? Or upstairs?' asked Ruth.

'I don't know.' Gracie felt like the room was spinning. 'George!' she called again, as she ran towards the main doors.

'Wait,' said Ruth. 'Over there!' She pointed to a large table of toys. George was hiding underneath.

Gracie turned back, her heart still racing as she made for the table.

She knelt and dragged George out. 'Don't ever run off like that again,' she scolded, her face flushing with anger.

George threw back his head and roared. 'Shut up! Shut up!'

'Calm down, George,' said Gracie. 'What's the matter?'

'They won't let you in the grotto if you make a scene,' added Ruth.

'I don't want to go in! That's why I ran! I hate Father Christmas. I hate him!'

'Shh, shh, it's all right,' said Gracie. 'Why do you hate him?'

'Tell us what the matter is,' added Ruth.

'I can't tell you! He made me promise,' wailed George between gulping sobs.

'Who did?' coaxed Gracie.

'He did,' George jabbed towards the grotto.

'*Father Christmas?*'

He gasped for air. 'I saw Father Christmas backstage damaging the aeroplane!'

Chapter Eighteen

An Eyewitness Account

'He must mean Natalya,' said Ruth. 'She was dressed as Father Christmas.'

George shook his head. 'It was a man. He had a big shiny toolbox and he was messing with the aeroplane. I had trouble getting my tutu to stay up, that's why I was late going on stage.'

Gracie gasped. 'George! Why didn't you tell me sooner?'

'Father Christmas told me to keep my eyes and mouth shut. He said if I told anyone he wouldn't deliver any Christmas presents this year. Then Molly and Mandy found me. I thought they were his evil elf helpers!'

'But the man you saw isn't the *real* Father Christmas. He's the saboteur!' Her mind swirled with possibilities. 'It could be Mr Chadwick? He is the only suspect who could easily pass for Father Christmas, and he has a toolbox, although he claimed it was now missing.'

'He looked like the real one,' said George, wiping his snotty nose on his sleeve. 'He was old with a white beard and them little glasses. He was wearing a red cape with a fur-trimmed hood.'

'That's why Natalya's cape disappeared!' said Ruth. 'The saboteur took it as a disguise.'

'Exactly. Anyone could pass themselves off as Father Christmas with a red cape and a fake beard, just like George could pass for a ballet dancer,' said Gracie. 'I bet fake beards are easy to get; they might even sell them in here.'

'They definitely sell them in the joke shop,' said George, looking a little brighter. 'I remember seeing them.'

'Mr Grime, my editor, got his costume delivered from there. I suppose Natalya had her cape specially made for the show.'

'She needed something quick to put on and that would go easily over her dance costume,' said Ruth. 'It would be just as easy for the saboteur to put the cape on over his ordinary clothes.'

'And he knew Natalya would have to get another one made for the show,' added Gracie. 'So people would think it was her if they saw him.'

'We still don't know why he's targeting the ballet. Perhaps he's an evil rival Russian ballet director?' said George. 'We need to make him confess.'

'Sergei the Saboteur,' said Ruth. 'What do you think Gracie?'

'Maybe,' She wasn't convinced.

'How are we going to trap him?' asked George.

Gracie was quiet for a minute while she thought. 'Our saboteur likes writing letters, doesn't he? What if we sent him a reply?'

'But we don't who he is or where to send it,' said Ruth, her brow wrinkling.

Gracie waved her copy of *The Gazette*. 'We could print it in the newspaper. I could switch one of the letters to Father Christmas on the Auntie Astra's page.'

'What are you going to put in the letter?' asked George, eyes wide.

'We need to lure him out and make him confess.'

'But he's dangerous,' said Ruth. 'And there's only a few of us.'

'We need to choose a place with lots of people,' said Gracie, 'or even better – lots of children!'

'But you *hate* crowds,' said George.

'Yes, but if we have the League around us then we'll be safe, and we can get everyone to help us catch the saboteur. We're going to invite him to the Blackpool Tower Christmas Eve Party!'

'It won't work,' said Ruth sadly. 'He won't be put off by an audience – he wasn't when he damaged the aeroplane.'

'We'll make it work. I'm going to come up with a plan that can't fail,' said Gracie.

'We have to try,' said Ruth, making the signal of the League of the Shining Star.

Gracie and George returned the hand signal.

* * *

Tibs, the pet shop, was further up the street. It overflowed on to the pavement with wooden rabbit hutches, parrot cages and kennels, all decorated with tinsel and big bows. Gracie, George and Ruth weaved around them and went inside.

The smell of sawdust and animals was really strong, and there was a cacophony of animal sounds. Woofs, miaows and snuffling from the dogs, cats and rodents, combined with the tweets and chirps from the aviary section.

'How can I help you?' squawked an African grey parrot from the counter.

'We're just browsing,' said Gracie.

'Actually, I'm here to choose something for Christmas,' said George. 'Are you for sale?'

'Cheeky!' replied the parrot.

'I'm not sure Ma wants any more animals at home though . . .' George continued.

'What were you thinking of?' asked Gracie cautiously.

'A snake, maybe.'

Ruth gave a squeal. 'They don't have snakes in here, do they? I hate snakes.'

Gracie glanced around. 'I don't think a snake is a good idea. Snakes eat rats. They swallow them whole.'

George gulped. 'My Fred wouldn't like that.' His eyes widened as he ran across to a cage. 'A monkey maybe!'

Gracie hurried after him.

George was peering in at a cute marmoset monkey.

'Thirty shillings!' said Gracie. 'No chance!'

They all made their way along the packed aisles. Little zebra finches and canaries fluttered from inside their cages, while hamsters and gerbils scurried into their dens.

'Let's see, I've already got a rabbit,' said George, dismissing the ones in the shop. 'And a budgie and two doves . . .'

'Sounds like a zoo,' said Ruth, giggling.

'Don't they have anything bigger?' asked George.

'What about a nice goldfish,' suggested Ruth, watching one swim around its bowl.

'I'd rather have a shark,' said George.

'I think they've sold out of those,' laughed Gracie.

'How about a terrapin?' suggested Ruth.

'Boring!'

'Hmm, well I don't know what else to suggest,' said Gracie.

George pointed across the shop at a woman behind a shelf

of dog food. 'I want one of those!'

The girls swivelled to see.

'A fox stole?' asked Gracie, wrinkling her nose.

'No!' He pointed again.

The woman had a small black and white terrier on a lead.

'I want a puppy,' said George, folding his arms.

'Well, a dog's better than a lion,' teased Gracie. 'Now, do we need to pick up some pet food while we're here?'

George nodded.

'I'm going to look at that parrot again,' said Ruth, trotting away. 'I want to teach it to sing!'

Gracie and George laughed, then made their way to the back of the shop. George scoured the shelves, picking out a bag of bird seed and a bag of rabbit food.

'I wish that was all I needed,' said a man's voice.

Gracie turned to see Albert Ramsbottom with a trolley full of animal feed.

'I want to be a zoo keeper like you when I grow up,' said George. 'Can I have a job?'

'You're a bit young.' Albert raised an eyebrow. 'I recognise you two. Aren't you the kids that found Molly and Mandy?'

'We are,' said Gracie proudly.

Ramsbottom's face was sour. 'And what were you doing poking your noses around backstage? Did you have anything to do with that girl's accident? I might have to report you to the Tower Management. They're looking for people who were acting suspiciously.'

'We didn't touch the plane,' said Gracie.

'I don't want to go to jail,' shouted George.

'Lucky for you I'm not the type to snitch.' He started to walk away, pulling the trolley. 'And if you *do* want to be a zoo keeper,' he called over his shoulder, 'remember this. Plenty of animals *look* tame, but they are still wild creatures. Get too close and they chomp your head off.'

Gracie stuck out her tongue as he walked away. 'Hilda was right. He really is horrid. Now let's pay for your food and find Ruth.'

'Can I teach that parrot a rude word?' asked George. 'Maybe it could learn to say Mr Sheepbum!'

Gracie giggled. 'I might just let you.'

* * *

Gracie rang the Mosson's doorbell. 'Here, blow your nose, George, and smarten yourself up a bit.' She passed him a hanky. The Mayfair was bigger and grander than their own boarding house.

Audrey opened the door. 'Oh! You've brought Ruth too! Come in. Come in.'

Gracie took off her mitten and woolly hat and stuffed them into her coat pocket.

'What's that stink?' asked George loudly. 'Are your guests having boiled cabbage for dinner?'

Gracie blushed.

Audrey laughed. 'That is my mother's miracle comfrey treatment. It might pong but it works wonders. My ankle is much better!'

'That is good news,' said Ruth.

Gracie reached into her bag and pulled out a card and the chocolate apple.

'Thank you,' said Audrey opening the envelope. She laughed and showed Ruth the design – a black terrier with a bandaged paw. 'I'll put it on the mantelpiece, then we can share the chocolate.'

'Oh no,' said Gracie. 'That's just for you.'

The hallway was lined with station signs and train photographs, with red and green paper chains strung over the top. She remembered now that Audrey's father was a station master; it seemed his profession was his passion.

They passed a china cabinet filled, not with special decorative treasures, but boxes marked Hornby. It reminded her of the ones she'd seen in Ted Lakin's toyshop.

'Wow!' gasped George as they stepped into the parlour.

Mr Mosson was standing next to a large model railway. 'I was just adding a new tunnel.'

Audrey placed the card on the shelf above the fire and the chocolate apple on the sideboard. Then she went over to the table. 'I've got some new greenery to put in place.' She leant over and added two small fir trees to the station. 'Father likes to make seasonal changes to his railway. We've got some tiny twinkling lights to put in next; and I've been painting some miniature carol singers to put on the platform.'

'It's so realistic,' said Gracie. 'I feel like I could hop on that train and go on a fantastic journey.' Violet would love this, she thought.

'Now, George, how about you and I take her for a run?' Audrey's father pointed to the black steam engine with brown and cream carriages.

He grinned. 'Yes, please.'

Mr Mosson placed a train driver's hat on his head, then blew his whistle. George carefully moved the switch to ON and the train began to move.

The engine followed the tracks out of the station, along green fields with cows and sheep, through a level crossing, in a figure eight. Next it passed under a footbridge, past a duck pond, through the new tunnel and finally back round to the station.

'Come through to the kitchen in the back, girls, let's leave the boys to play,' said Audrey's mother, appearing at the doorway. 'I've made a fresh pot of tea.'

* * *

Mrs Mosson placed three iced gingerbread men on to a plate in the centre of the kitchen table. The aroma of spices and fresh baking filled the air. Gracie broke off a piece of biscuit and popped it into her mouth. 'Hmm, delicious, Mrs Mosson.'

'Scrumptious,' added Ruth.

Gracie bit the head off hers.

'I'll take some through for the railway staff,' Mrs Mosson said with a wink.

'So, tell me,' began Audrey, once they were alone. 'Is it true what it says in *The Gazette*? Did Natalya really crash in the aeroplane?'

'Not exactly,' said Gracie. 'She got stuck above the stage and one of the cables snapped, but luckily the other held. Natalya was really shaken up, though.'

'How terrifying! I got a letter from the Tower, of course, saying the show's cancelled. I bet everyone's devastated.'

'*Angry*,' corrected Ruth. 'The saboteur must think he's been so clever.'

'He? You know who it is then,' added Audrey, sitting up. 'Go on, tell me.'

'We only know it's a man,' said Gracie. 'A man disguised as Father Christmas, and we have a plan to catch him. We're going to put a letter in *The Gazette* to lure him to the Christmas Eve Party.'

'A letter? What, like an invitation?' asked Audrey.

'We haven't decided yet,' said Ruth.

'What if he doesn't see the letter, or ignores it?'

Gracie breathed heavily out through her nose. 'You're right. We need something else . . .'

They ate their gingerbread while they thought it over.

'I've got it!' said Gracie, suddenly. 'We should put on one more show! A special *Winter Belles* performance at the party. That's bound to lure the saboteur out.'

The girls clapped with excitement. 'What a brilliant idea! That's sure to get our phoney Father Christmas rattled.

'Now, what about the toy shop set?' asked Gracie. 'When does it get dismantled?'

'The stagehands won't take everything apart until after New Year,' replied Audrey. 'Let's hope they've not made an early start, what with the show getting cancelled.'

'Fingers crossed,' said Gracie. 'Music?'

'I'll ask my pa,' said Ruth, brightly.

'We'll need costumes too,' added Gracie.

'They'll have been locked away until next season,' Ruth explained. 'All the storeroom keys are in the caretaker's room. We'll have to sneak in when Chadwick is out of the way.'

'Excellent. I think you've thought of everything,' said Audrey.

'Not quite,' said Gracie. 'There is one more hurdle. Madame Petrova. Without her permission, the Tower Management will never allow us to put on the show.'

Chapter Nineteen

A Confession

Audrey and Ruth had suggested Gracie ask Frances to pay a visit to Madame Petrova. They'd given her the older girl's number and, after explaining their plan, she had arranged to meet her the next morning.

'Ready?' asked Gracie, raising her fist to knock on Madame Petrova's.

Frances nodded. 'But remember, let me do the talking.'

Gracie knocked three times. They had already agreed that the ballet director was more likely to listen to one of her cast.

After a minute, footsteps, and the tap of Madame's cane on parquet floor, echoed as she neared.

The door opened slowly. Madame peered around the wood. 'Frances! What are you doing here?'

Gracie gave a friendly smile, as the ballet director's gaze fell on her.

'We wanted to ask after Natalya,' Frances replied. 'All the girls are really worried about her.'

Madame closed her eyes and rubbed the bridge of her nose as though easing a headache.

'Perhaps, we could see her? Just for a moment,' prompted Frances.

'It is rather cold,' said Gracie quietly.

'Is it?' Madame gave a little shake of her head and her eyes widened, as though finally taking in her surroundings. Freezing fog had turned the sky white.

Frances stepped forward. 'You don't want to let cold air into the house, not while Natalya is recovering.'

'My daughter is . . . asleep,' said Madame, shuffling backwards.

'What a shame,' said Frances, stepping inside. 'We'll leave her a note for when she wakes, then.'

Madame Petrova clutched her cane and led them down the hallway. 'You'll have to be quick.'

Gracie pulled out her notebook and followed. It wasn't much warmer inside. The hallway was wide enough to take a small unit with a telephone and a coat stand with two fur coats on it. She undid the buttons on her own woollen coat but didn't ask to hang it up. She had a feeling they wouldn't

be staying long. Frances had whipped off her hat and checked her reflection in the wall mirror, as she fixed her short black hair.

The girls followed Madame into a little brown room with two mismatching armchairs and a worn wooden coffee table. There was a small Christmas tree in front of the window and a handful of cards of the mantelpiece.

Madame's hands shook as she leant her cane against the fireplace and stoked the dying embers with a poker.

'We won't be a minute,' Gracie rested her notebook on the table, took off her glove, then pulled out her pen and began to write.

Madame Petrova lowered herself into the chair by the fire. She tapped her fingers on the armrest.

'Christmas in Blackpool must be very different to Russia,' began Frances.

Madame Petrova barked a laugh. 'Christmas is banned in Russia.'

'Banned?' repeated Gracie, pausing from her writing.

'Why?' gasped Frances.

'Because, in Communist Russia, celebrations must be secular, not religious. The royal family had been in charge for 300 years. Then came war and famine. People were angry that they had so little while the Tsar had so much.

'There was a revolution. The monarchy was abolished.

Lenin and the communists took power. They promised peace, bread and land. My country changed its name, it's leader – yet I fear nothing will change for ordinary people.'

'Is that why you left?' asked Gracie.

'I left for Natalya. I do everything for Natalya.' She gave a deep sigh. 'I knew we had to leave but I didn't know where we would go. I wished and wished for a sign. Days passed; weeks. And then, just as I had given up hope, I received a letter from England. An invitation to come to Blackpool and take over *Winter Belles*.

'You ask about Christmas in Russia. When I was a little girl, we would be visited by *Ded Moroz*. Grandfather Frost is an old man with a fur hat and coat and a long white beard who brings well-mannered children presents.'

'Just like Father Christmas!' gasped Frances.

'Exactly. Only Ded Moroz doesn't fly through the sky on a sleigh pulled by flying reindeer, he travels in a three-horse carriage – a *troika*!'

'That was the name of the music used in the overture, at the start of the show,' said Gracie.

'Here was my sign at last.' Madame Petrova's face crumpled. 'But I was wrong. Life is not a fairy tale. Wishes aren't granted. Dreams don't come true.'

'But you *were* right,' said Frances. 'You *are* meant to be here and put on the show.'

'It's not your fault there have been accidents. It's the saboteur!' exclaimed Gracie.

'*Saboteur?* Please, not that nonsense again.'

'It's not nonsense, Madame,' Frances insisted. 'We have an eyewitness who has seen them!'

'My brother saw the saboteur meddling with the aeroplane before your daughter got in it. He was wearing a Father Christmas cape so, if anyone saw, they'd think it was Natalya.'

'There is no man; no mysterious saboteur,' said Madame, standing unsteadily. 'Finish your note. I want you to leave.'

Gracie frowned as she finished her message. They had been waylaid. They were supposed to be getting Madame's permission to put on one more show. She had to convince her that the saboteur was real, even if it meant telling her about their plan to trap him. She took a deep breath. 'I know you don't believe there is a saboteur, but your dancers do, and, what's more, we have a plan to bring them to justice.'

Madame turned to face the wall. She said nothing for a minute.

Gracie looked to Frances, who shrugged in confusion.

Finally, the director spoke, her voice a whisper. 'There is *NO* saboteur.' She turned around. 'It was Natalya. All of it.' She reached into her dress pocket and pulled out a folded piece of white paper and passed it over.

Gracie unfolded it, her eyes scanning the words quickly.

Dear Mama,

I am sorry I hurt Audrey. I meant for the scenery to fall on myself. I only wanted to find a way to leave Winter Belles. I thought if I hurt myself then I wouldn't have to dance any more. I will never be as good as you, and I'm tired of trying to be. I only hope that you will continue the show with the other girls.

Your loving daughter,

Natalya

Gracie ran her thumb over the embossed image of a British bulldog. It was the same branded paper as that used by the saboteur.

'You're sure this is Natalya's handwriting?' She passed the letter to Frances.

Madame wiped her eyes and stumbled out her words. 'It is a little shaky, but my daughter is very unwell. She frightened herself more than she planned, I think.

'I suppose I pushed my daughter too hard. I wanted her to be a great ballerina like myself. I didn't realise Natalya was unhappy. Unhappy enough to try and stop the show at any cost.'

Gracie pictured Natalya in the aeroplane, screaming for help. That had been genuine fear. The confession must be false. 'The letter could be forged.'

'I know it isn't. Natalya *is* responsible.'

Frances shook her head. 'I still can't believe she is the saboteur.'

'It is a matter for the Tower Management, not you girls. Frances, I know Natalya is your friend, but the best thing you can do is forget about the whole thing.'

'If we could speak to Natalya, just for a minute or two,' said Gracie.

Madame's bottom lip trembled. 'No one can speak to her. She is very sick. The doctors have sedated her.'

Gracie tore out the page from her notebook and passed it over. 'When she is awake, please give her this. We would like to say goodbye properly. My home telephone number is on it.'

'When Natalya wakes, we will be leaving Blackpool,' said Madame Petrova. She sighed, 'but I will pass your letter to her.'

The girls stood up and followed Madame to the front door.

Frances hesitated in the hallway by the coat stand and pulled on her hat. She brushed against the fur coats. Gracie's eyes widened as her friend slipped a hand into a pocket and pulled out a set of keys. Frances lifted a finger to her lips.

'Thank you for your time,' said Gracie, her voice feeling squeaky. Relieved Madame's back was to her, she turned the catch on the lock.

'Yes, thank you,' said Frances, finally at Gracie's side again.

* * *

'I can't believe you stole Madame's keys!' scolded Gracie, once they were outside.

'I haven't stolen them, I've borrowed them,' said Frances with a shrug. 'We need to find evidence to prove that Natalya is innocent – unless you believe that rubbish about her being the culprit.'

'No, of course I don't.'

'Well then,' Frances pulled out the keys and dangled them. 'These will get us into the changing rooms and Madame's office.'

'All right,' Gracie sighed. 'But only because I feel sorry for Natalya. She's been through so much – it was bad enough the saboteur tried to hurt her and has caused her to have a breakdown, but now they're framing her too!'

'They are really twisting the knife,' agreed Frances.

'Did you notice the *confession* was written on the same type of paper as the poisoned pen messages? I'm certain the saboteur sent it. I know that letter's a lie, but I don't know how we can prove it.'

'It was cleverly done. It fooled her own mother,' said Frances.

'But we can be clever too,' replied Gracie, tucking her hand deep into her pocket as they walked down Adelaide Street, past boarding houses and on to Bank Hey Street. All the shops were closed and the street was deserted, except for the occasional seagull parading past.

'I know. We'll use the saboteur's own trick to catch him.'

Frances grinned. 'Tell me more.'

'The saboteur must have copied Natalya's handwriting to fake her confession. We need to find an example of Madame Petrova's writing so I can fake a letter to the Tower Management. The Children's Ballet *will* perform at the Christmas Eve Party.'

Chapter Twenty
A Spanner in the Works

Madame Petrova's office was on the same floor as Natalya's dressing room. Frances found the right key, and they snuck inside. Luckily, there was no one about.

Frances turned on the light while Gracie went straight to the desk. On top of it was an in tray, a letter rack, a pen pot, a desk lamp and a framed photograph of Natalya.

She flicked through the letter rack.

'Anything?' Frances asked, leaning over her.

'All letters *to* Madame, nothing written by her. I suppose that's to be expected.'

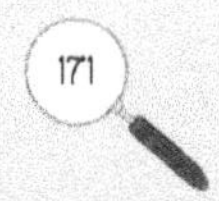

Frances pulled open the desk drawer. She pulled out a writing pad of pale apricot paper.

'May I?' Gracie tore off the top sheet and held it to the light. 'This could work!' She placed the paper on to the desk and took a pencil from the holder. 'George showed me how to do this once. It was in one of his comics!'

Pressing her left elbow on to the sheet to keep it steady, Gracie scribbled over the paper in pencil. The grey began to reveal invisible writing. 'When you write on a notepad, the sheet underneath picks up the indentations. You wouldn't notice it normally, unless you were looking closely. The pencil highlights all the words so they're visible. See!'

She showed the letter to Frances. 'The saboteur could have used the same technique to get an example of Natalya's handwriting.'

'Want me to try copying Madame's handwriting? I think I could do a good job.'

'Yes, please,' Gracie passed over another unused piece of paper. 'There's something else about this paper. I've seen some like it before and I think it's important.

'It's different to the paper used by the saboteur . . . Oh, of course! It's the same apricot paper as the letter to Father Christmas . . . but that doesn't make sense. Madame Petrova wouldn't be asking Father Christmas to be a ballerina.'

Did Natalya use her mother's paper? Gracie wondered. That

was possible, but the content still didn't make sense.

She realised Frances was staring at her; her face was bright red.

And that's when it struck Gracie. 'Frances, did you send a letter to Father Christmas?'

Frances bowed her head. 'You must think me very babyish, but I kept seeing all the children's letters in *The Gazette.* It sounds silly, but I wrote one of my own. I even got as far as Lakin's Toy Shop, but I swear I never actually posted it. I was too embarrassed; I hid it on a shelf and hurried away.'

The letter must have ended up on the floor and got trodden on. 'It couldn't do any harm asking Father Christmas to make your wish to become a star come true,' said Gracie.

'That's what I thought. I asked Natalya for some paper, thinking it might be lucky. Only there's been nothing but bad luck since.'

Footsteps sounded heavily in the corridor.

'Someone's coming,' said Frances.

Gracie yanked her friend's arm. 'Quick, get down!' She pushed the chair out of the way and crawled under the desk.

Frances squeezed in next to her.

Gracie squidged up. '*Oof!*' she cried, her knees smacking against something cold and hard. Her eyes widened. It was a metal toolbox. Could it be Chadwick's lost one? And, if so, what was it doing in Madame Petrova's office?

'Who's left the light on?' said a man's voice. Keys jangled as whoever it was tried to unlock the door. 'That's funny, it's not locked.' The door opened, and Neville Chadwick stepped into the room.

'Madame?'

Gracie sucked in her breath as the caretaker turned off the light.

They were plunged into darkness. Every sound was exaggerated. The door scraping across the floor as Mr Chadwick closed it, the key scraping into the lock.

Frances wriggled. 'That was close.'

'*Ssh*,' whispered Gracie, 'I think he's still outside.'

Suddenly more footsteps sounded further away.

The caretaker called out 'Who's there? Show yourself!'

'It's only me, Neville,' called another man. 'Actually, I was looking for you.'

Gracie adjusted her elbows, trying to get comfier. Frances was pressed up tight against her. She reached out to touch the toolbox and tried to pull it closer. A trickle of sweat ran down the back of her neck.

'Oh! I thought you were an intruder, Harry!' said Mr Chadwick. 'I've been on high alert since the accident.'

'I thought they would have stepped you down, now the show's been cancelled.'

Gracie's heart pounded. Why didn't they move on?

'No, I'm all right, I've still got to do my patrols.'

'Well, get on with them,' whispered Frances.

'What about you though, Harry? Will they pay you for the rest of the run?'

'I'm all right. I got paid upfront. Mind you, I've got to spend a chunk of it on a train ticket,' said Mr Linnet. 'I'm off to London!'

London, Gracie mouthed silently.

'What've you got to go to London for?' asked Mr Chadwick.

Mr Linnet's voice was full of excitement. 'A music publisher is interested in one of my songs!'

'Oh, Harry! That's fantastic!'

'I know! I hate to say it, after what happened to Natalya, but the show getting cancelled has got me out of a bind. You see, I've to meet them in person. I told Madame Petrova that I'd ask Mrs Waters to play in my place for a couple of evenings – but she didn't like that idea one bit! She said I was contracted to work, and that was the end of the matter.'

Gracie's mouth fell open. *So that's why they'd had a disagreement at the dress rehearsal!*

'Only now the show's cancelled, there's nothing to stop you,' said Mr Chadwick.

'Well, there is one thing. That's why I was looking for you. I've got a train to catch in an hour – it will be a whistle-stop trip. I'll be back in time for Christmas. But I need someone I trust to look after Ruth while I'm away. She always loved staying with you and Gladys.'

The caretaker hesitated. 'Ah, but I've turned into a bit of a grouch since I've been on my own. My cooking's not up to much either . . . Couldn't you ask one of the other girl's mums?'

Frances wriggled again. Gracie tried to squidge up to make more room. Her back was aching from being on all fours.

'Please, Neville. She'll be no trouble; she spends all her time practising the piano or listening to music in her room. You could stay on for Christmas itself, Miriam and Nora are coming.'

'Oh, go on then!'

'Brilliant – I'll tell Ruth to expect you. I'll leave my key with her.'

'Right you are,' replied Mr Chadwick. 'Come on, I'll see you out.'

At last, thought Gracie.

They waited for the men's footsteps to fade. Then clambered out from under the desk.

Gracie stretched her back and rubbed her left elbow.

Frances flicked the desk lamp on.

Gracie bobbed down to pull out the toolbox.

'Gosh!' said Frances. 'Do you think Madame Petrova is the saboteur!'

'No,' replied Gracie. She lifted the toolbox on to the desk and examined it closely. 'There's no obvious fingerprints on it, in fact I'd say it's been polished recently.'

'Ooh,' said Frances. 'Open it up!'

Gracie undid the catch and opened the lid, pulling out the contents. There was a hammer, two screwdrivers, a chisel, a spanner, a sprocket set, a tape measure and a stubby pencil.

'Look!' A small piece of white fluff was caught on the end of the screwdriver. Gracie felt it between her fingers and then passed it to Frances.

'It's like cotton wool.'

'Exactly, like the material used for Father Christmas's beard or fur trim.' Gracie stroked her chin. 'The letter, the toolbox, they're all being planted so we won't identify the real culprit. The saboteur is obviously confident finding his way around the Tower.'

'And now he is trying to put the blame on Natalya, but we know the truth.'

'And, best of all, he doesn't know we're on to him.' Gracie put the tools back into the box. 'Now, let's finish that letter and then we can push it under the Tower Manager's door.'

Chapter Twenty-One
Good News

The town centre was teeming with workers hurrying to Blackpool's offices and shops. Monday was the coldest day yet, with another morning frost, and Gracie took her time climbing *The Gazette*'s glistening steps.

She made her way to the newsroom, her mind full of the wording for a replacement Father Christmas letter for Auntie Astra's page – a letter she hoped would lure the saboteur to the party.

Gracie settled herself at her desk, put fresh paper into her typewriter and began to strike the keys.

Dear Father Christmas,

Please can I have some new ballet shoes for

Christmas? I am a ballerina, and on Christmas Eve I will be dancing in a special performance of Winter Belles *at the Blackpool Tower's Children's Party for members of The League of the Shining Star.*

Best wishes

Natalya Petrova

Gracie ripped the letter out of the typewriter. Then, heart thudding, she walked across the newsroom to the subs desk.

'Mr Emberton wants to swap one of the Father Christmas letters,' she said, trying to keep her voice steady.

The man groaned. 'Comps won't be happy,' he said, but he still took it.

Gracie walked back to her desk, breathing a sigh of relief. She couldn't believe she'd done it. If anyone found out that she'd lied, she could lose her job.

'Good morning,' bellowed Mr Grime, as he entered the room. 'Shall we have an editorial meeting?'

Reporters grabbed their notebooks and hurried into the conference room. 'Come on,' said Ava. 'You're part of the editorial team too. We've got to show the men we're just as good as them – better in fact!'

Gracie grinned. She and Ava were the only females on the editorial staff. She trotted after her colleague. Could she persuade Mr Grime to give her a permanent job? And what would Ma say if

she told her she preferred working at *The Gazette* to The Majestic?

'What big stories have we got lined up for the Christmas Eve edition?' asked Mr Grime, sucking on his pipe. He pointed to the man on his left.

'I'm doing a round-up on shop insurance premiums going up,' replied the reporter.

'Very Christmassy,' said the editor, rolling his eyes. He pointed to his neighbour.

'I've got some police court hearings – mainly speeding cases. The bench wished everyone a merry Christmas before giving out their fines.'

Mr Grime groaned. 'Not exactly festive. Next.'

'I'm writing a piece on how the fog and ice has put a dampener on trade.'

'Really? Is that what our readers want the day before Christmas? Go on then. It will make a lead, I suppose.'

'I'm doing slippery paths – residents are demanding more sand be spread in town.'

'Has anyone got anything positive?' sighed Mr Grime, stroking his beard.

'I've a nice piece on how sales assistants have been remarkably good-tempered considering the weather disruption,' said Ava.

'That's more like it – we can use an illustration of ladies in lovely hats to go with it. Thank you, Ava. Anyone else?

What about you Miss Fairshaw? Please tell me you've a winter wedding up your sleeve.'

Gracie spoke quietly. 'I've got a story about a lemur being saved from prickly porcupines at the Tower Menagerie.'

Mr Grime guffawed. 'That's more like it. That's what readers want. Funny stories. Heart-warming tales. John, ring the hospital – they'll be having a Father Christmas visit to the children's ward; I want photos. Michael, I want an update on the Opera House pantomime. The rest of you, think festive! Go on. Off you go!'

Everyone jumped up.

'Hold on, Gracie. I want a word with you.'

'Yes, sir?'

'I was impressed by you in the meeting. We need a lead for page three. I want you to go back to Lakin's Toy Shop. Ted has some news, but he wants you to have the exclusive. Apparently, you made quite an impression on him.

'Write up your porcupine story first, then see what you can find out. You might as well call in at a few shops on your way, we could do with some colour to put into Jack's story on shop sales. He writes like an accountant!'

* * *

The sales assistants were so busy that they didn't want to talk. Instead, with their agreement, Gracie watched shoppers making their purchases.

She was gathering quite a picture of Christmas 1935 for *The Gazette*'s readers. She began with food. At Rainford's Butchers, turkeys were scarce, so people were opting for ducks and geese instead. She wondered if Ma had thought to order ahead?

She was amused to see that Roberts' Oyster Bar was advertising that no Christmas dinner was complete without oysters. She couldn't imagine George wanting to eat those – he wouldn't even try sprouts!

Then on to gifts. In Boots the Chemist, Gracie watched customers buy bottles of perfume, eau de toilette, brush sets, toilet cases and powder puffs. *Blackpool folk will be smelling sweet in the new year!* she thought, with a grin.

Time was getting on. It would soon be lunchtime and she had asked everyone to meet her at one o'clock. She should get to Lakin's.

She stalled at *The Gazette* stationery shop, thinking Mr Grime would like it if she included the newspaper's own shop in the write-up – and she had another reason for popping inside.

Gracie approached the salesgirl and took out her press card again. 'I'm writing an article about Christmas gifts.'

'Oh, yes. I can spare you a minute. What do you want to know?'

'What are your best sellers, please?'

'Hmm, fountain pens are very popular, as are propelling pencils. I've sold a couple of whist sets, and diaries and calendars are doing well too, of course,' replied the salesgirl.

'What about letter-writing sets?'

'Oh yes, we've a new range in with tulips on; sell like hot cakes!'

'Do you stock British Bulldog paper?' asked Gracie. 'I've been trying to get some of their blue, for my uncle.'

The salesgirl smiled. 'Oh, we sell lots of it. Men are a bit more boring when it comes to their choices, aren't they?' She opened a drawer under the sales counter. 'Is this the one?'

'Yes, that's it,' said Gracie, taking out her purse. 'Thank you.'

* * *

Having bought the stationery set, Gracie continued to Lakin's. She was shocked to see a queue snaking out of the toy shop. Then an awful thought came to her. *I hope they've not gone bust!*

Gracie approached a mother with two little boys in the queue. 'Excuse me, is Lakin's having a closing down sale?'

'Hardly! It's having a boom. Shop's never been so popular!'

'Really!'

'Oh yes. I didn't even realise Lakin's was still in business till I read about it in t' *Gazette.* I hadn't been in since I was a little girl, and, well, it hasn't changed a bit! It's wonderful. So nostalgic – and you get proper customer service too. The boys loved it too – they insisted we go back again today!'

Gracie blushed. Her story had turned things round for Ted! She had to see for herself! She took out her press pass and went to the front of the queue.

The shop front was in the process of being repainted, but still in its traditional livery.

The window gleamed and a brand-new display of classic toys had been staged. There were big jars of marbles, skipping ropes, spinning wheels and a glossy dappled-grey rocking horse with red reins right in the centre.

Gracie pushed open the door and stepped inside. The whole shop smelt of pine and lemon. There wasn't a scrap of dust to be seen. The aisles were brimming with happy families picking out gifts. One man demonstrated how to do tricks with a yo-yo, while a mother showed her daughter a beautiful china doll.

But the biggest surprise was behind the counter. There was Mr Lakin, looking much younger and happier. His shirt was perfectly ironed, and his suit looked brand new.

'I'm so glad you could come, Miss Fairshaw. Your article prompted so many new customers. We haven't been as busy in years. It spurred me on to tidy up the place – well, and myself. I told Mr Grime what a marvel you are, when he called in to collect the last of the Father Christmas letters. He said he'd send you over to write a follow-up article!'

'It would be my pleasure,' Gracie replied, beaming.

'Oh, and Gracie, if you ever need anything in return, you only have to ask!'

'There is one thing actually . . .' she leant in and whispered in Ted's ear.

Chapter Twenty-Two

The Show Must Go On

Gracie had arranged to meet everyone at a small café on Victoria Street, close to the Winter Gardens.

They placed their orders for soup and potato cakes at the counter, then sat around a long rectangular table with padded-bench seating. Gracie squeezed in next to Frances, while Ruth and Audrey sat opposite.

Gracie brought everyone up to date with all that had happened, including how evidence had been planted to frame Natalya.

'How will we convince the Tower Management to let us put on one more performance without Madame's support?' asked Ruth.

'That's all sorted. Madame has given her approval,' she

fibbed. 'I explained how important the Christmas Eve Party is to the children of Blackpool and what a treat it would be for them to see a performance from the Tower Children's Ballet. She could hardly say no to that.'

Frances grinned. 'No one wants to be a Scrooge!'

'Will Madame Petrova and Natalya be coming to the party?' asked Audrey.

Their presence would certainly help lure out the fake Father Christmas. 'Hopefully, if Natalya is feeling well enough,' replied Gracie.

'There's still one problem,' said Frances. 'It won't be much of a show with only two dancers.'

'*Three*,' corrected Audrey. 'My ankle's much better and as we're only doing a short routine, it'll be a good test.'

Two matching duffel coats were approaching their table from the counter.

Gracie stood up. 'Ah, here they are!'

The duffel coats were untoggled and hoods lowered revealing Tom and Violet.

'Hello, did you miss us?' asked Violet, hugging Gracie.

'She missed me,' said Tom, putting down his tray. 'She was probably glad to have a rest from your incessant chatter.'

Violet poked her brother with her elbow.

'Violet and Tom are going to help us catch the saboteur,' explained Gracie.

'I'm going to do a tap-dancing reindeer solo! I'll be a hoofer,' Tom joked.

Audrey laughed loudly. 'You're so funny!'

Tom beamed.

'What about music?' asked Frances. 'Ruth's pa might not get back in time to play.'

'He did say he would do his best!'

'I could ask my big sisters,' said Audrey. 'They're in a band. I sometimes play my saxophone with them.'

'Saxophone?' said Tom, 'That would be amazing.'

'Excellent. So, shall we go over what happens at the Christmas party?' asked Violet. 'You won't have been, Gracie, but I presume you girls have?'

The dancers nodded.

'They open the doors at midday,' said Tom. 'There will be around 200 children invited. They will be welcomed into the Ballroom for party games . . .'

The others talked over each other.

'Pass the parcel,' said Frances.

'And musical chairs,' said Ruth.

'And charades,' said Audrey.

'There's a buffet too,' said Violet. 'The usual sandwiches, savouries and something sweet for afters.'

'There's loads of fizzy pop and chocolate too. Everyone stuffs themselves!' added Tom.

'Everyone's energy drops after the food, so that's when the brass band comes in; it's usually the Salvation Army. I love hearing them play the traditional carols,' Ruth added.

Audrey nodded. 'The last song is always 'Good King Wenceslas'; that's the cue for Father Christmas to arrive.'

'Mr Grime, the editor at *The Gazette* will play him. I'm one of his elf helpers,' explained Gracie. 'I'm going to stick really close to Mr Grime, in case the imposter tries to switch places with him.'

'We don't want the fake Father Christmas putting itching powder in his costume, or anything,' agreed Violet.

Gracie stared at her. 'I've just remembered, George and I went to the joke shop and asked if he'd sold any itching powder. He joked that Father Christmas had been in, doing last minute shopping, but now I think he might have meant it!'

The waiter appeared with a tray of tomato soup, bread rolls and potato cakes. Gracie breathed in the rich smell. She was starting to feel a little warmer.

'Who do you think Father Christmas really is?' asked Ruth. 'Have you any idea?'

She couldn't tell Ruth that her pa was one of the remaining suspects. He had been backstage around the time the prop plane was sabotaged and he had a motive. 'I haven't enough concrete evidence yet,' said Gracie, dipping her bread roll into her soup. 'That's why we have to catch them in the act.'

Chapter Twenty-Three

The Night Before Christmas

The Tower Ballroom swarmed with children of all ages. Everyone was wearing their Sunday best. The girls in velvet dresses of red, purple or navy blue – some with bows, others with white lace collars. The boys in matching smart trousers and blazers, most with a tie. Everyone's shoes were polished and gleaming. Hair had been brushed and combed.

Gracie's elf outfit had been on the big side, but Ma had pinned it in at the back and rolled up the sleeves. She checked her reflection in the mirrors on the ballroom wall. At any other time, she would have laughed at the elf hat and two beetroot-juice circles on her cheeks, but she was too worried to be amused.

Coloured paper chains had been hung along the walls and a golden throne had been placed in the centre of the ballroom for Father Christmas to sit on.

All the presents had been taken off the huge Christmas tree and sorted into two piles; one pile for girls and one pile for boys. Gracie and her friends had added a special third pile; all in green paper and provided by Ted Lakin that morning.

Gracie would flex her hand in and out to make the signal of the League of the Shining Star. Any child who replied with the signal would get one of those presents.

Some grown-ups were organising all the children for party games. Sitting them in several circles on the floor for pass the parcel. George was among them.

She looked round the room. Was everyone in position? She'd told George to join in the party games, she felt sure he'd be safest there. Violet was going to manoeuvre around the ballroom keeping an eye on Mr Linnet. Gracie would keep an eye on Mr Chadwick and watch out for anyone else who might be the saboteur.

There he was! The caretaker was dressed in overalls, but had added a Father Christmas hat in an attempt at festivity. He was making a beeline for Nora Waters, a small parcel wrapped in brown paper in his hand.

Gracie steered a course towards them, pausing when she was within ear shot.

'I made it for you,' he said shyly.

Mrs Waters peeled back the paper. 'Oh Neville, I absolutely love it!'

It was a beautiful marquetry box. Cream pieces of veneer had been painstakingly applied in diamonds on the sides and the lid was decorated with a pair of ballet shoes inlaid in mother of pearl. It was stunning.

Mrs Waters gave him a big hug.

* * *

The games passed off without incident. Now it was time for the buffet. Gracie, Violet and George joined the long queue that had formed leading to several trestle tables laden with food. As she got nearer, Gracie could see sandwiches cut into triangles, cheese and pineapple on sticks, pickled onions, pork pie wedges and sausage rolls. There were also bowls of crisps, jellies, tiers of fairy cakes and plate upon plate of mince pies.

'We could start a food fight when we see the saboteur,' said George, his eyes on a huge trifle with glacé cherries.

'Don't you dare!' Gracie scolded. 'We aren't doing anything that would ruin this lovely party.'

'Lots of these children have been looking forward to this for a long time,' Violet added.

'Yes, we're not going to spoil it for them,' agreed Gracie.

They filled their plate with delicious grub, then found a space to sit and eat. The food was lovely, but Gracie felt too

anxious to really enjoy it. Then she spotted the Petrovas coming into the ballroom.

She hurried over to greet them.

'Well, Miss Fairshaw. We are here as requested,' said Madame Petrova, her arm protectively around her daughter.

'Thank you for coming,' said Gracie.

Madame gave a curt nod. 'The girls are waiting for you backstage.'

Gracie felt a sense of unease as they walked away. Had she done the right thing inviting the Petrovas? She knew them being at the party could help draw out the fake Father Christmas, but what if it prompted a fresh attack?

She was distracted by the rousing sound of a brass band. The Salvation Army marched into the ballroom in their smart uniforms, their instruments shining brightly.

They gathered near the stage and performed a trio of Christmas carols, finishing with 'Good King Wenceslas', just as Audrey had said.

As the song concluded, Gracie saw Mr Chadwick switch on an extra-large electric fan near the ballroom entrance. He then threw handfuls of fake snow into its gyrating blades, creating the effect of a light blizzard.

'Ho, ho ho!' called a loud, cheery voice, as the doors to the ballroom opened once more.

The children began to squeal in delight.

Sleigh bells tinkled as two donkeys in red harnesses pulled a beautiful gold sleigh inside. Mr Grime waved a white gloved hand at all the children. 'Merry Christmas! Merry Christmas!' He looked magical under the ballroom lights in his padded-out red velvet suit.

Gracie breathed a sigh of relief and crossed the room, trying not to trip in her over-sized Elf slippers.

Mr Grime got out of the sleigh and made his way to the throne. His black boots were so polished that they shone.

The children formed an orderly queue, giddy with excitement.

'Ho, ho, ho! And here is my faithful elf!' Gracie stood next to a huge tower of wrapped presents.

The first child stepped forward nervously. He looked about George's age.

'Hello young man,' said Mr Grime in a deep voice. 'What would you like as a present this year?'

'A model boat, please, Father Christmas,' said the boy shyly.

'Well, I will see what I can do.' Mr Grime nodded at Gracie. 'Now, would you like a surprise present from me now?'

'Yes please, Father Christmas.'

Gracie made the League of the Shining Star signal and the boy returned it. She picked up one of the green presents. 'Remember not to open it until the reindeer finishes dancing then wait for the shining star signal,' she whispered.

'That's a nice touch giving out special presents for members of the League,' said Mr Grime.

A girl of about five was next. She looked even more nervous. She was a bit too young to help with the plan. Gracie didn't make the signal.

'And what's your name?' asked Mr Grime.

'Martha,' replied the girl.

'And what would you like for Christmas?'

'Some colouring pencils, please, Father Christmas.'

'I'll do my best. Now, would you like a surprise present too?'

'Yes please.'

She handed out a present wrapped in tartan paper.

Next was a boy of about eight. He didn't make the signal either, so he got a tartan-wrapped present too.

After that, she barely listened to the youngster's requests, instead concentrating on making the signal if the child was old enough.

She handed over a parcel to a small boy with thick glasses who had returned the signal. 'Yes, yes, wait for the signal. I heard you.' He snatched the green gift out of Gracie's hand.

'What's he upset about?' asked Mr Grime.

'I've just been telling them not to open their presents until later,' replied Gracie. 'He didn't like having to wait.'

* * *

An hour later, all the gifts had been distributed. She must have given out nearly fifty green presents.

'Father Christmas is ready for his glass of sherry,' said Mr Grime. 'Thanks again for your help, Gracie.'

It would soon be time for the *Winter Belles* performance. Red velvet seats had been laid out in rows facing the thick stage curtains. Gracie told George and Violet to keep watch from seats at the back, while she positioned herself near the front.

She looked to the piano, as Mr Linnet began to play 'Joy to the World'.

Gracie glanced around the ballroom, looking for any man acting suspiciously.

'Oh, hello again!' said a voice with a Liverpudlian accent.

She turned to see Lin, the waitress from the Oriental Lounge, and Hilda, the zoo keeper, taking the seats next to her.

'Hello,' said Gracie.

Lin wore a lovely yellow dress, while her friend was dressed in a white blouse and plaid skirt.

'I can't believe Ramsbottom gave me the afternoon off,' whispered Hilda to her friend. 'It must be Christmas!'

A hush fell across the room as Mr Linnet began to play the piano.

The stage curtains opened revealing the toy room set with the nesting Russian matryoshka dolls.

Madame Petrova strode out into the centre of the stage. Her cane tapping slowly against the wooden boards.

'Boys and girls, I am delighted to announce a special performance from select members of the cast of *Winter Belles* and some special guests.'

Everyone clapped enthusiastically.

Gracie's whole body tensed. Surely the saboteur would make his move soon. She scanned the eaves of the stage. Where was he? She wanted to get up and look around herself, but she couldn't cause a disturbance in the middle of the act.

'Firstly – something a little different! Ready Prancer?' Madame stepped to the side of the stage. At least the ballet director was close by, should something happen suddenly. That cane of hers would make a good implement.

Gracie looked at the windows. They all looked secure. The aeroplane prop had been removed. There were large toy soldiers; would they be safe? Could the saboteur have set a booby trap?

Tom bounded on to the stage, dressed in a furry brown all-in-one with antlers on his head.

He beamed with joy as he shuffled and heel-stepped on the spot, the metal taps on his shoes' heels and toes making a fantastic rhythm sound.

'Isn't he good,' said Lin.

'Yes, very,' said Gracie. She glanced around, looking for signs of the saboteur.

'Is something wrong?' whispered Hilda.

She shook her head. 'I'm looking for Father Christmas.'

'I can't see him,' said Lin.

Tom finished his routine and bowed. At once the Shining Star children began to tear off the green wrapping paper around the gift from Father Christmas. There was pop guns, skipping ropes, balls, bow-and-arrow sets and cat's cradles. Ted Lakin had provided everything Gracie had asked for.

Gracie relaxed. The saboteur would be attacked by dozens of children if he tried anything now.

She drew in her breath and waited for Madame Petrova to announce the next performer.

'Christmas is a time for togetherness. The Blackpool Tower Children's Ballet have faced several challenges this season, but all our struggles make us stronger. United, we overcome. Boys and girls, please show your appreciation for our next piece, performed by our talented soloists, Frances Ashton and Ruth Linnet.

The audience cheered and clapped.

The girls appeared from the corners of the stage.

Mr Linnet began to play 'The Holly and the Ivy'. Frances and Ruth danced across the stage in soft green dresses; floral wreaths in their hair.

Gracie felt her body relax as she enjoyed their beautiful routine – their movements in perfect harmony with the gentle carol.

* * *

The ballet dancers wafted into the wings to rapturous applause. Madame Petrova walked slowly into the centre of the stage once more, but this time she was not alone. Her arm was around Natalya. 'My daughter and I are unable to dance this evening, so instead we would like to sing a traditional Russian song for you – it is called 'The Forest Raised a Fir Tree'.'

Dozens of girls filed in from the wings. They were all dressed in white leotards and tutus. It was the entire children's ballet!

Mr Linnet began to play the piano.

Madame Petrova and Natalya sang in Russian, as the girls linked arms and swayed from side to side.

Gracie linked arms with Lin, and soon the whole audience swayed arm in arm.

'A little fir tree was born in the forest . . .' Madame began to translate the words, as though reading a beautiful poem. 'It was straight and green, in summer and winter. The frost is packed around the roots, while the blizzard sings its lullaby. Sleep dear spruce, sleep tight!

'A timid rabbit hops by, beware the angry wolf!' continued Natalya. 'Hush! Listen! Here comes the woodcutter. His sledge slides over the snow. The old man has chopped down the little fir.'

They finished together. 'He has dressed the fir tree and brings it to us for the holiday. See how happy the fir tree makes the children.'

The audience applauded.

Suddenly Mr Linnet stood up. 'If I may interrupt proceedings . . .' he sprinted towards the stage. 'Excuse me, Madame,' he said as he stepped up to the microphone. His face was bright red. He looked around the room anxiously. Beads of sweat on his brow.

A shiver ran down Gracie's spine. *What was happening?*

Chapter Twenty-Four

Under the Mistletoe

Madame was smiling, she waved her hand towards the stage steps in encouragement.

Mr Linnet addressed the audience loudly. 'The next song you will hear is one of my own. It is called, appropriately, 'My Winter Belle', and I am very excited to announce that my composition is going to be published!'

Gracie joined in with the applause.

'Mrs Waters has very kindly offered to play it for you.'

Gracie twisted her head. The former director was indeed sitting at the piano.

'Today is a very special day,' Mr Linnet continued. 'And there is one person here who could make it extra special – Miriam Waters. Miriam, please would you come on to the stage.'

Everyone scanned the room for the former star.

She was seated a few rows back. She stood up and made her way to the front of the ballroom. Somehow, she even managed to make a Father Christmas hat look stylish.

Mrs Waters began to play. The music made Gracie picture falling snowflakes and crystal-clear icicles.

'Miriam, I have a question to ask you.'

She smiled at her mother, then turned back to Harry Linnet. 'I would love to sing your song.'

He blushed. 'Well, that would always be nice, but . . . er . . . actually, I had a different question . . .' He dropped on to one knee and held out a small box. Something twinkled inside. 'Miriam, *you* are my winter belle. Darling, will you marry me?'

'Oh, Harry! Yes! Yes! Of course, I will!'

Mr Linnet stood up and slipped the diamond ring on to Miriam's finger. Then he reached into his pocket and pulled out a small bough of mistletoe and held it above her head.

She leant forward and they kissed.

The audience awwed.

Gracie could feel tears brimming.

Lin was weeping quietly. 'A Christmas proposal is so romantic!'

As the couple embraced, Mrs Waters stood up and cheered, and Mr Chadwick called out, 'Well done, old man!' from the side of the stage.

Madame Petrova beamed. She stood straighter and made one last walk to the centre of the stage as Harry and Miriam retreated arm-in-arm.

'Boys and girls, I am delighted to announce a special finale to our show. I give you Audrey Mosson as 'The Christmas Fairy'.'

Gracie clapped as Mrs Waters continued to play beautifully. Perhaps the saboteur had been put off by the expression of Harry and Miriam's love. Had all the talk of Christmas appealed to his better nature? She truly hoped so.

A single spotlight fell on to the stage, illuminating the figure of Audrey as she flew across on an invisible wire, her iridescent fairy wings shimmering. She seemed weightless and ethereal as she danced over the stage. Every movement was perfectly timed to Harry Linnet's composition.

Gracie settled into her seat, allowing herself to relax and enjoy her friend's enchanting performance.

Audrey finished with a series of pirouettes in the air. Spinning like a cyclone, then falling gently to the stage.

The audience broke into loud applause.

Audrey stood and curtsied, then raised her arms to welcome the rest of the performers on to the stage.

Tom, Audrey, Frances, Ruth and Natalya came out to the front and stood next to Madame Petrova, before bowing their thanks to the audience. The *corps de ballet* crowded in behind.

The audience were on their feet, cheering.

'That was wonderful,' said Hilda.

'Absolutely wonderful,' concurred Lin.

'Yes, wasn't it,' agreed Gracie, blowing hot air into her fringe with relief. *Everything is going to be all right*, she thought.

'Ho, ho, ho!' called a voice from the wings.

Gracie tensed as Father Christmas strode on to the stage, his face hidden behind a large bouquet of red roses.

Gracie leant forward, her skin tingling. Was it Mr Grime or the saboteur?

What should she do?

The audience sat down again as Father Christmas crossed to Madame Petrova and leant into the microphone.

'Ho, ho, ho!' he repeated, turning face on.

His Santa hat was pulled low over his eyebrows. His beard covered the rest of his face. She still couldn't be sure. But wait, that beard – it was too white, a bit thin and wavy. It wasn't perfectly groomed like Mr Grime's. The beard was false; the Father Christmas was a fake.

It was the saboteur!

Gracie could sense the League children in the audience also leaning forward. Out of the corner of her eye she saw some raise their toy weapons.

Father Christmas grabbed Madame Petrov by the waist and yanked her, screaming towards the right wing.

'Mama!' cried Natalya, lurching after her.

Father Christmas snarled and shoved the dancer hard. She stumbled back into Frances and Ruth, who were right behind her.

'Let her go!' cried Tom.

Suddenly, George leapt up armed with a bow and arrow. He pulled back and fired at the saboteur. 'Bullseye!' He cried, as the arrow sucker knocked off his Father Christmas hat, revealing his bald head.

The saboteur roared savagely as he rubbed his face, letting go of Madame, who ran towards her daughter.

Gracie turned to the audience, thrusting her arm into the air, making the sign of a Shining Star. 'Now!'

Tom, Madame and the dancers fell to the floor in perfect timing as the stage was bombarded by flying jacks and marbles.

Gracie cheered as more League children stood and aimed their pop guns, catapults and bows and arrows at the saboteur.

More missiles fired through the air. Lumps of plasticine, stones and pellets pelted Father Christmas. They scrambled over the seating – some threw balls with perfect aim, while others were set on tying up the villain with skipping ropes and cat's cradles, as the fake Father Christmas stumbled off stage.

Tom crossed to the microphone. 'Stop!' He made the shining star signal again.

The children lowered their weapons. The girls curled their fists in frustration.

'You did it. He won't dare try to hurt the Petrovas ever again,' said Tom.

Gracie hoped he was right. *Have we done enough?*

Everyone cheered.

'But he got away,' said George, jumping up and down in frustration.

'Yes, but at least there were adults here to see that the saboteur is real. We can relax now, knowing that the police will have to be involved,' said Violet.

Mr Linnet and Mr Chadwick, Miriam and Mrs Waters had started to clear the room, ushering out the children, telling them to wait outside for their families. A few League members refused to go, wanting to discuss their bravado with their friends.

Gracie was quiet. She was still trying to work out who the saboteur was. Violet was right, the police would probably capture him but she would have liked to have been the one who unmasked him.

'Who was that?' Hilda's eyes were like saucers.

'That was the man who has been trying to ruin this year's Children's Ballet,' said Gracie.

'It's true that someone's been targeting the ballet then?' gasped Lin. 'I thought that was just a rumour.'

'I'm afraid not. There has been a series of attacks . . .' she continued, trying to catch her breath.

'He put itching powder in Natalya's costume,' said Violet. 'She's the prima ballerina.'

'How awful!' said Lin.

George wiped his nose on his sleeve. 'And he sabotaged a piece of scenery which fell on our friend Audrey's leg.'

'She's lucky she can still dance,' said Violet.

'And you don't know who did all these nasty things?' asked Hilda.

Gracie shook her head. 'The saboteur tried to blame Natalya, but we know it's not her. He sends anonymous poison pen letters, using cut out newspaper letters.'

'What did the letter say?' Lin asked, her brow wrinkled.

'You are not wanted here . . .' Gracie began.

'*Leave or you will regret it?*' finished Lin.

Gracie gasped. 'How do you know what it said?'

Lin clasped a hand to her face. 'Because I was sent a letter too.'

Chapter Twenty-Five

The Hunt

'I thought I was being forgetful at first,' Lin explained. 'My apron went missing, then my keys. Then two days ago, I found someone had put maggots in with the cakes and left the letter on the side.'

'This isn't just about the ballet,' realised Gracie. 'Think about the words. You are not wanted here. Leave or you will regret it. What if the saboteur thinks his victims shouldn't be in England? The Petrovas are Russian.'

'And I'm of Chinese heritage,' said Lin.

'What's that noise?' asked Gracie.

A hole opened in the centre of the stage and the famous white Wurlitzer rose into view.

'It must be a surprise encore,' said Hilda.

Gracie had a bad feeling.

The organ's low notes were being played in a haphazard manner. Instead of Reg Dixon at the keys, it was Mandy and Molly!

The remaining League children started to laugh.

'Oh, thank goodness!' cried Gracie. 'It's just those naughty chimps again.'

One was jumping up and down on the foot pedals, while the other banged her fists on the three keyboards.

Hilda, Lin and Gracie ran to the Wurlitzer.

'Look at the state of them,' said Hilda. 'Their hands are covered in jam. They must have broken into the tea party supplies.'

There were sticky handprints all over the Wurlitzer.

'Come on, Molly, playtime is over.' Hilda scooped up the keyboard-playing chimp.

Lin picked up Mandy.

Gracie bit her lip as she studied the messy marks. 'I didn't realise chimpanzees have fingerprints like us,' she said. An idea forming in her mind.

'Oh yes,' replied Hilda. 'Apes, monkeys and even koalas have them, and they are individual, just like human ones. The chimps are always leaving sticky fingerprints on my clothing. It was paint, the other day.'

Gracie remembered the fingerprints on the poison pen letter.

'Could the chimps have been trained to deliver the letters.'

'They could be taught to do anything, they are very clever,' replied Hilda.

The final pieces of the puzzle were falling into place. 'And has anyone else at the Tower been made to feel unwelcome because they are foreign?' asked Gracie.

Hilda nodded. 'I'd forgotten all about it. Isn't that awful! You remember I told you about the snake escape. Well, the Around the World exhibit also had this bazaar – a kind of shop selling crafts made by people from different countries; it was a long white counter with a canopy above. It had all these treasures on it; beautiful rugs and tapestries, lovely lanterns, silver plates, beautiful boxes and wooden animals. A few months after the python got out, someone went up there and smashed everything up. They scrawled on the front of the bazaar counter in black paint. The message said "Go Home. You're Not Wanted Here".

'Not long after Around the World was closed and now the space is used by Fredini and his dance band for concerts.'

'Did they find out who did it?'

Hilda shook her head. Something about her face told Gracie she knew more than she was saying.

'But you had your suspicions, didn't you?' said Gracie, suddenly realising who the bald Father Christmas was. Of course, she had recognised him! 'It was Albert Ramsbottom, wasn't it?'

George whistled. 'Not Mr Sheepbum!'

The girls shushed him.

Hilda covered her face. 'I found a tin of paint hidden in the back of the feed storeroom a few days later. It was ordinary black paint, so I couldn't prove anything, but I *knew*. He's always saying rude things about anyone who isn't white British like him. I told you he was horrid, but I swear I never thought he would try to hurt people.'

Gracie swallowed hard. Ramsbottom had chosen British Bulldog writing paper and spent hours cutting out his vile messages of hate. She remembered him now, with his wheelbarrow full of animal bedding. There had been straw and piles of old Gazettes.

'I don't know why I never considered Ramsbottom.' A memory flashed into her mind. 'He wears a toupee, doesn't he?'

George sniggered.

Hilda nodded. 'That's why I sometimes tell him to keep his wig on when he's cross! He doesn't think anyone knows, but you can see it move when he adjusts his cap.'

'The chimps haven't been escaping, he's been letting them out so they could deliver his poison pen letters.'

Molly the chimp shrieked! She jabbed a jammy finger towards the ballroom balconies.

Mandy began to shriek too.

Hilda's face turned as white as the Wurlitzer. The chimps

wriggled and shrieked as she walked awkwardly down the stage steps.

Gracie looked up – her heart gave a hard thud of panic.

A deep guttural roar echoed out from above.

'Stop! Everyone stay where you are,' Gracie called.

'Is that a *lion*?' asked George, in awe.

'Ramsbottom's released Wallace!' Hilda clutched Gracie's arm. 'It's the python all over again!'

'I'll raise the alarm,' said Lin, hurrying down the steps.

'Use the Tannoy. Say it's a Code DANIEL,' called Hilda, as Lin burst out through the staff door next to the stage.

Gracie's head swirled at the thought of an escaped lion.

'There!' Violet pointed at the top balcony. The black tip of a long tail swished and flicked. 'We need to evacuate everyone calmly before he gets any closer.'

George's mouth fell into an O. He yanked himself free and lunged into his jacket pocket. 'I've got just the thing!' It was a small red-and-white-striped box marked STINK BOMBS. 'I got them on Saturday from Jokes Galore.' He tore open the packaging. There were three small glass vials inside.

'Wait,' cried Gracie, as George threw it on to the ground. The ampoule shattered on impact, releasing a gag-inducing stench.

Gracie felt sick, as she pulled at George's arm. Too late, he dropped the second stink bomb.

Another wave of nausea hit Gracie. Her eyes watered. Her throat burned.

'I've still got one left, if we need it!' George waved the last vial at her.

'Don't you dare!' Gracie spluttered, between coughs.

The other children ran pell-mell towards the exits, wailing.

'You mustn't run! If you run, Wallace will come after you,' cried Hilda, but her voice was lost in the screams.

There was a movement in the balcony. Gracie got a glimpse of blond mane. 'He's heading for the stairs.'

'I need someone to take the chimps back to the menagerie for safety,' said Hilda. 'I'm going to see what's left of the buffet to try and tempt Wallace. He hasn't got much left in the way of teeth, but his claws are still deadly.'

'I'll do it,' said Violet.

'George can show you the way,' said Gracie. 'I'll help Hilda.'

* * *

Gracie and Hilda ran over to the buffet. They pulled apart sandwiches and sausage rolls and began to lay a trail of meat treats for the lion.

'Let's hope this works,' said Gracie.

Hilda crossed her fingers. 'Come on, we need to get to the stage.'

There was a crackling sound and Lin's voice echoed into the ballroom.

The girls paused.

'This is a public announcement. The Tower Management have ordered the immediate evacuation of the Tower. This is not a test. Please remain calm. There is no need to panic. All staff please follow procedures for *Code DANIEL*. Hilda, Gracie, if you can hear me, help is on its way!'

'We could try to drop the stage curtain and use it as a barrier,' said Gracie.

'There isn't time,' said Hilda. 'We need to get out of here, now.'

Wallace was padding lazily down the stairs at the back of the ballroom.

Gracie shuddered. She'd forgotten how big he was.

Hilda took Gracie's hand and led her slowly towards the stage.

They both kept one eye on Wallace as they crept up the steps.

Hilda pointed to the wing.

They swivelled and edged nearer.

'And where are you going?' called Ramsbottom from stage left.

Gracie and Hilda froze.

'Children shouldn't be sneaking around and poking their noses into things that don't concern them,' scolded Ramsbottom. 'I'm going to have to put you both on the naughty list.'

Gracie caught a glimpse of movement behind the matryoshka dolls.

'And after I'd already chosen your Christmas presents. I've

got you some . . .' Ramsbottom picked up the smallest Russian doll '. . . Skittles?'

The doll shot across the stage, almost catching Gracie's leg. She just managed to spring away in time.

'Are you all right?' asked Hilda, eyes wide.

'I think so – *Look out!'* Gracie pulled her new friend aside as two more, bigger, matryoshka bounced across the floor.

They jumped out of the way.

Gracie could hear her own breathing as Hilda pointed to the fourth doll. Ramsbottom was wrapping his arms around it's middle. He heaved at the head half until it finally pulled free like a cork. 'How about spinning tops?' He sent the doll top cascading across the stage.

Gracie and Hilda leapt apart as the bottom half came spinning towards them.

They bent over, trying to catch their breath.

Ramsbottom was already behind the next doll. 'Or how about dominoes?' he grinned as he pushed hard against the fifth matryoshka.

It toppled precariously and rocked into the sixth, bigger doll so it was soon tottering too.

Gracie and Hilda ran forward and tried to keep the dolls upright, but they were too heavy.

The girls staggered back, as the two matryoshka slammed onto the floor with a sickening bang.

Ramsbottom's laugh reverberated. 'I'm going to smash you to smithereens and then Wallace can eat what's left of you.'

'We've *got* to get off this stage,' Gracie urged.

Hilda shook her head. 'That will put us straight into Wallace's path.'

'There's nowhere else to go!' cried Gracie. But Hilda was right, the lion had eaten the trail of snacks and was now strolling towards the stage.

Gracie scanned round. The wings were blocked off by fallen dolls. They were definitely trapped!

'Up here!' shouted a voice. It was Tom!

'Oh, thank goodness!' Gracie cried, looking up. There was Frances, Ruth and Audrey, too. They were holding the flying harnesses.

'We're going to lower these down to you,' called Frances. 'Put them on and we'll winch you to safety.'

Wallace halted and began chuffing. He looked ready to charge.

Gracie's heart raced as the harnesses were lowered to them. Time was running out!

She and Hilda stretched up to grab them.

'Got them!' They called, before quickly fastened each other into their harnesses. Their fingers fumbling with fright.

Ramsbottom was groaning with effort as he shoved with all his might against the seventh and biggest matryoshka.

Hilda checked all the buckles were tight. At last, they were securely strapped in.

'Now!' called Gracie, wincing as the final doll jolted.

Ramsbottom took several steps back and ran forward, arms stretched out.

They were being lifted!

Tom winched and winched.

'It's working,' cried Gracie as her feet left the ground.

'We're going to be all right!' cried Hilda.

Ramsbottom rammed himself against the matryoshka, but it was just too heavy.

He turned round slowly, eyes glaring, and roared.

Then he lurched to the centre of the stage, arms trying to clutch at Hilda and Gracie's feet. Trying to pull them down.

Gracie kicked out her leg, in a beautiful ballet arabesque, smacking her foot into the zoo keeper's clean-shaven face.

'Ouch!' cried Hilda.

Gracie kicked again. Smack into Ramsbottom's jaw. He gave a tumbling pivot and fell to the ground.

The girls were winched higher and higher. The platform was just inches away.

Suddenly, Wallace gave a deep roar, that made the hairs on Gracie's neck stand up.

Gracie gasped as she looked down. The lion was at the bottom of the stage steps.

Ramsbottom clambered to his feet and staggered to the toy shelves at the back of the stage, knocking off teddy bears and porcelain dolls as he tried to climb out of the way. He snivelled for help.

Frances and Ruth helped Gracie on to the platform, high above the stage while Tom and Audrey helped Hilda.

'Isn't there another harness?' Gracie asked, unbuckling herself. 'I know Ramsbottom's awful, but we've got to try and rescue him!'

The lion placed one paw on the first step and roared again.

Tom was urgently winching Gracie's harness down.

Ramsbottom lay face down on the floor. He pleaded snottily over and over as the lion crept up the stage steps.

The harness wafted in the air above Ramsbottom's head.

'Grab it!' called Hilda.

He's frozen with fear,' said Gracie. 'There's nothing we can do.'

'Wallace!' called a familiar voice from the balcony. It was Lin! And she was holding a huge joint of meat. She must have got it from the Oriental Lounge kitchen!

'Dinner time,' She hollered, lobbing the meat over the edge. It landed with a thud on the ballroom dance floor.

The lion turned his head and sniffed the air.

Wallace licked his lips and swaggered towards the joint, his tail flicking. Then he lay down, set a paw on top of the meat and began to gnaw lazily.

'Phew,' said Gracie.

'Albert,' hissed Hilda. 'Albert, get up! For goodness' sake! Get up!'

But Albert Ramsbottom could not be stirred into action.

Chapter Twenty-Six

Stop Press

'He's been! He's been!' cried George, gently shaking Gracie awake. 'Come and see!'

Gracie rubbed her eyes and stretched. It was still dark outside. Her first Christmas Day in Blackpool. It would feel very different to the one in Milltown where she'd grown up.

She got out of bed, adjusting her nightie and throwing on her dressing gown. Her mind churning over last night's events.

Help had arrived just in time for Albert Ramsbottom. Wallace had been captured by the Tower Circus's lion tamer and taken back to his enclosure.

Hilda had been offered a temporary promotion to manage the menagerie – and she'd immediately hired Lin as her assistant.

It seemed very unlikely that Ramsbottom would ever return to Blackpool Tower.

Gracie stepped into her slippers and padded through to the Fairshaw's living room. Two woollen socks hung from the mantelpiece above a roaring coal fire. George bounced up and down next to his. 'I can't wait to see what I've got!'

The kettle whistled across the way. Ma was making a special Christmas morning breakfast of kippers.

George and Gracie raced each other into the kitchen and sat down at the small table just in time for Ma to dish up.

They tucked into their grilled fish on toast, washed down with hot tea, while Ma put the turkey into the oven.

A pile of potatoes, carrots and parsnips were on the side, waiting to be peeled later, along with a stalk of Brussels sprouts. Gracie had offered to help as Phyllis was spending Christmas morning with her parents.

'Let's leave the dishes for later,' said Ma, putting their plates into the sink. 'I want to see you open your presents.'

They filed through to the living room. George passed Gracie her stocking first, then pulled down his own. They lay the socks carefully on the floor and spent ages carefully unwrapping their gifts. There were satsumas, a bag of nuts, a chocolate apple and sugar mice.

At the bottom, George found a yo-yo and a clockwork elephant. 'Brilliant!' he proclaimed.

Gracie was delighted to find a fountain pen and a frog-shaped brooch with diamanté eyes.

'Time for family gifts,' said George, shuffling on his knees to reach under the Christmas tree.

He checked the labels on the parcels and passed them out.

'I wonder what this could be,' said Ma with a grin, picking up a cylindrical shaped present. She peeled back the wrapping. 'Well, I never, a stick of Blackpool rock! What a clever present, George.'

'It's minty,' said George, 'so you won't need to brush your teeth tonight.'

She opened the present from Gracie next. 'My, what a lovely scarf – just my colour.' Ma held the red knit next to her face. 'It will keep me nice and warm an' all.'

There were more presents; a box of Turkish delight from the Hill sisters, a bottle of sherry from next door and a family soap set from a Great Aunt, which made George groan.

There was a Playbox story annual for George and a copy of *Anne of Green Gables* for Gracie.

The doorbell rang.

'It's a bit early for visitors, isn't it?' said Gracie.

'Well, let's go and see who it is,' said Ma, a twinkle in her eye.

* * *

'Mr Emberton, do come in.' Violet and Tom were grinning either side of their father, who was holding a large parcel. There was a picnic basket by their feet.

'This is yours, Gracie,' said Mr Emberton. 'I'll carry it inside for you. It's very heavy.'

Tom picked up the basket. 'This is for you, George. We've had great fun hiding it at our house.'

'Come inside, out of the cold,' said Ma, leading them to their private quarters at the rear of the boarding house.

Mr Emberton looked relieved to put down Gracie's parcel on the kitchen table. Ma blushed, apologising because she'd left the dishes, but no one else cared. She filled the kettle and offered round a plate of Christmas cake with thick marzipan and icing.

Gracie slowly tore off the brown paper, revealing a black case with a handle.

It was a portable typewriter! She gasped with surprise. Gracie opened the case and ran her fingers over the round glass keys. 'Is it really for me?'

'You like it then?' asked Ma. She smiled at Violet and Tom's father.

'I love it!'

'It's not brand new, but everything works as it should,' Ma added.

'It's perfect.'

Tom lifted the basket on to the table. 'Right, your turn.'

'Isn't it a bit chilly for a picnic?' George asked, confused, as he lifted the lid.

A creamy head poked out. A snuffling black nose sniffing the air.

'A dog!!! I got a dog!' he cried, lifting out the pup. 'It's a boy,' he laughed, as it piddled on him.

'He's a Fox Terrier,' said Mr Emberton. 'A very proud breed. He'll need lots of looking after.'

'I'll walk him every day and brush him and teach him lots of tricks.'

'He needs a name before any of those things,' said Ma.

'I'm going to call him Skippy,' said George.

'Skippy will need his breakfast,' said Ma, 'and don't forget *all* your pets need feeding too.'

* * *

It was time for Christmas Dinner! The hallway brimmed with people, waiting to go into the dining room. The Hill sisters were giddy with excitement as they led the way.

For one day only, The Majestic's guests would dine alongside staff and family friends. The tables had been covered in red tablecloths, with placeholders, napkins and golden crackers at each setting.

Gracie looked round at the boughs of holly and mistletoe. Taper candles flickered, and there was a scent of orange pomanders in the air as everyone found their seat.

Serving dishes had been filled with roast potatoes, boiled

potatoes, vegetables, pigs in blankets and stuffing. The turkey had been carved into slices, and everyone took turns helping themselves to meat from the platter or passing the gravy boat along.

Phyllis and her parents had been invited too, of course, it was a tradition at The Majestic, but there were first-timers too. Violet, Tom and Mr Emberton. Madame Petrova and Natalya, Lin and Hilda. George was slightly disappointed they hadn't brought Molly and Mandy along.

Mr Emberton told everyone how well Gracie was doing at *The Gazette*, while Violet announced with glee that Mr Chadwick had offered her an apprenticeship.

The dinner was delicious. Cooked to perfection. Everyone told Ma so, and the Christmas Pudding with brandy sauce received a cheer when she brought it into the room.

Crackers were pulled – party hats donned, mottos shared – and stories told.

'You never finished the story of what happened to the python?' said Gracie.

Hilda grinned. 'They found it curled up round a bundle of clothes. It must have been trying to keep warm. There was a big story in *The Gazette*. Everyone thought they would close the pit down, but the very next day there was a huge queue of visitors, thrilled at the idea of walking across the snake pit containing the now-famous snake. It was brilliant publicity.'

'I'm not sure the Tower Management will want the public to know they had a lion on the loose!' added Lin. 'Though rumours are already flying round Blackpool that Albert Ramsbottom was eaten by a lion!'

Later, everyone withdrew into the parlour for the King's speech and a game of charades.

'And now, as a final treat for our guests,' said Gracie, hearing a knock on the door. 'If everyone could please put on their coats and step outside.'

'What's going on?' asked Elspeth.

'I don't know,' replied Edna.

Gracie grinned 'Ladies, I'd like to announce an exclusive performance of extracts from *Winter Belles*.'

The Hill sisters applauded. 'But the show was cancelled!'

'Postponed,' corrected Madame Petrova. 'The Tower Management have decided to extend the festive season with another two weeks of performances!'

'That's wonderful news,' said Gracie.

Natalya undid her wrap dress to reveal a silver leotard. Audrey, Ruth and Frances took off their coats to reveal their own.

They raised their arms above their heads and began to dance.

'This has to be the best Christmas yet,' whispered Edna to Elspeth.

And Gracie Fairshaw had to agree.

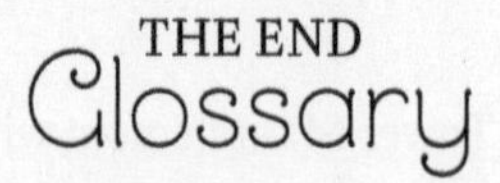

THE END
Glossary

BALLERINA: The principal ballet dancer.

BLACKPOOL GAZETTE: *The Gazette* began life as a weekly newspaper in 1873 and was started by Alderman John Grime. *The Gazette* became a daily/evening newspaper in 1929 and has also been known as the *West Lancashire Gazette.*

BLACKPOOL TOWER: Blackpool Tower opened to the public on 14th May 1894 and was inspired by the Eiffel Tower in Paris. Although it has changed internally over time, some key features survive, including the Tower Ballroom, the Tower Circus and the Tower Ascent (lift).

BLACKPOOL TOWER MENAGERIE: A collection of wild animals that were put on exhibition for the public from 1873–1973.

BOARDING HOUSE: An old-fashioned name for a guest house or bed and breakfast.

COPY: Pieces of writing/stories for a newspaper.

CORPS DE BALLET: The group of dancers who are not soloists.

CUTTINGS: Articles cut out of newspapers and kept as an archive.

DANCE BAND: A group of musicians that played the popular music of the 1930s for dancing to. There was often a band leader and guest singers.

EDITOR: The boss of a newspaper.

ELECTORAL REGISTER: A list of all the people in an area who are entitled to vote.

HEADLINE: The heading at the top of a news story that summarises the content.

LANDLADY: The owner and manager of a Boarding House, who would often have House Rules that set out what was allowed and not allowed.

LAYOUT: How a newspaper page is designed.

LEAD STORY – The main article on a page in a newspaper.

LEAGUE OF THE SHINING STAR: *The Lancashire Gazette* newspaper's Blackpool Edition included a regular children's page called 'The League of the Silver Star' written by Auntie Stella. Blackpool children were invited to send in letters and enter competitions and would receive a certificate once they joined up.

MATRYOSHKA DOLL: Wooden Russian dolls of decreasing size that stack inside each other.

NIB: An abbreviation for News in Brief. A short news article often in a column on the edge of a newspaper page.

PRESS PASS: Identification card for journalists including their name and photograph.

POZHALUYSTA: English translation of the Russian word for please.

SHORTHAND: A system for rapid writing using abbreviations and symbols.

STOCK PHOTOGRAPH: A picture used again and again of a person or place.

SUB-EDITOR – A person who checks that articles written by a reporter read well, are grammatically correct, have no spelling mistakes and are factually correct.

TYPEWRITER – A manual machine with keys for producing inked alphabetical letters, etc. on paper.

WURLITZER ORGAN – Designed by Reginald Dixon himself, the Wurlitzer Organ is still a very popular attraction of The Blackpool Tower Ballroom, with large crowds regularly dancing to its unique sound. This iconic instrument rises out of the stage floor and has over 1,000 pipes and 154 keys!

Historical Note

Gracie Fairshaw and Trouble at the Tower is a fictional story set in Blackpool at Christmas, 1935.

Blackpool is famous for its Tower and its many attractions. These have changed with the fashion over the years, but some features have survived from the early days – the Ballroom, the Tower ascent and the Circus. In the 1930s, the tower had lots of animal attractions. The aquarium on the south side of the ground floor was older than the tower and was incorporated into the build. It had cave-like walls and large glass tanks full of fish and other sea creatures. It closed in 2010.

Directly above, on the next level, was the entrance to the menagerie. This included an aviary and monkey house. Animals on display included lions, tigers, bears, panthers, porcupines, sloths, lemurs, leopards, hyenas, birds and reptiles. While the circus had their own animals, including horses, lions, tigers, polar bears, sea lions and elephants.

The menagerie closed to the public in 1969 with animals transferred to the new Blackpool Zoo near Stanley Park in 1977. The circus stopped using animals in 1990, but the stables and pens still survive in the basement.

The Roof Gardens were another floor up. This was where Bertini (actually a Londoner called Bert and the inspiration for Fredini) and his dance band performed. The Around the

World exhibit is made up but was inspired by the tower's Indian Village.

The Indian Village included a bazaar, and performances from musicians. The men played instruments from Bengal, including a harmonium – a bit like an accordion, a big stringed instrument called a sitar, and drums. There were also hypnotists, jugglers, magicians and nautch dancers too. The girls wore beautiful head scarves and skirts in jewel colours. The boy acrobats would climb up tall bamboo poles, right up to the glass roof, while carrying baskets on top of their heads! And a python really did escape one day!

Blackpool Tower Children's Ballet really did exist, although I have moved their show to Christmas time!

The Tower Ballet began in 1902, when Madame Pauline Rivers put on shows in the Ballroom featuring adults and children. The adult shows were less popular, so the performances soon featured children only.

The girls were professional dancers paid (poorly) for their work, but many of the dancers went on to have successful careers, including Audrey Mosson, the 15-year-old Railway Queen who switched on the Blackpool Illuminations in 1935.

Every season, hundreds of girls would audition for a place, with queues reportedly wrapping around the tower and along the promenade.

The most famous Tower Children's Ballet dancer was 'Little

Emmie'. Her real name was Emma Tweesdale and she was just eight years old when she first performed in 1908.

Both Madame and Little Emmie appeared on sheet music, and postcards were sold featuring the dancers. Little Emmie was also nicknamed 'La Petite Pavlova' after Anna Pavlova, the famous Russian ballerina.

One local story about Little Emmie is that for one show she appeared in a prop aeroplane suspended from the ballroom ceiling. The man in charge of winching her down forgot and went home! Little Emmie was left dangling, singing song after song, until help could be found!

Madame Rivers went on to adopt Little Emmie. Sadly in 1935 Madame Rivers died and Little Emmie retired.

A new ballet producer and teacher was found – Annette Schultz – and new rules were brought in. You now had to be 12 years old, and the girls were supervised by matrons or 'aunties' who would make sure they behaved and dressed appropriately. Another rule was that you couldn't speak to any of the Tower staff.

The Tower Children's Ballet's final show was in 1972.

Author's Note

I have always wanted to be a writer. When I was at primary school, my favourite lessons were the ones where my teacher would say, 'Today I want you to write a story about . . .'

I loved writing so much that I decided I wanted to start a school newspaper with my friends. My teacher thought it was a good idea, but she said instead of a newspaper we could have a pinboard to put up our stories. My mum had some bright yellow baseball caps from work with WAP on them – and so Wigan's Amazing Pinboard was born! By the time I'd finished secondary school I had two ambitions – to write books and to be a journalist! I did my first work experience when I was 17 at the *Wigan Evening Post* and the *Wigan Reporter/Observer*. I loved being given articles to write and overcame my shyness – soon I was ringing up strangers for quotes. I went on to study journalism, film and broadcasting at Cardiff University (the first in my family to go). About six months after graduating, I got my first job as a trainee reporter at the *Ormskirk Advertiser*.

I still have some old cuttings; I wrote all kinds of stories – about prize-winning pigs, market stall holders that sold large knickers, lots of magistrates' court hearings, parish council meetings and my favourite, education stories from schools for the Learning Zone pages!

I had a wonderful news editor called Clifford Birchall, who

taught me how to write a good news story – and pointed out my spelling mistakes and other errors.

I had to learn shorthand, become a good typist and learn all about media law and ethics.

One of my favourite tasks was to go through old copies of the newspaper from the 1960s and finding interesting stories to reprint as a Looking Back feature. I guess I was always interested in history!

Looking through old copies of the *Blackpool Gazette* helped me find the inspiration for my second Gracie Fairshaw book – and led to my decision to make Gracie a cub reporter!

Hopefully, her new career will lead to many more adventures!

Acknowledgements

Thank you to everyone who has read and recommended Gracie's first mystery – I hope you enjoy her second adventure in Blackpool!

A huge thank you to everyone at UCLan Publishing, especially Hazel Holmes, Becky Chilcott, and Charlotte Rothwell. Much love also to the Uclan MA publishing students and Alexa Gregson-Kenmuir.

Yet again, I am delighted to thank Jenny Czerwonka who has designed and illustrated a beautiful book cover for Trouble at the Tower.

Thank you to Kathy Webb for her marvellous editing skills and Antonia Wilkinson for publicity and promotion.

Thank you to everyone at Bounce marketing, Get Blackpool Reading and all the booksellers, bloggers, journalists, reviewers and librarians who have supported Gracie.

Thanks also to Tony Higginson and all the lovely schools who welcomed me for (virtual) author talks.

A big cheer for SCBWI and hugs for all my friends, but especially Georgina Blair (beta reader extraordinaire,) Anna Mainwaring, Catherine Whitmore, Faye Sunderland, Mel Green, Louise Jones, Barbara Henderson, Ruth Estevez, Dom Conlon, Marie Basting, Dan Brockington and Marion Brown.

Thank you to the staff of The History Centre, Blackpool for assisting with my research into the ballet and the Gazette.

I would also like to thank John Davies-Allen and Heather Mardell for answering my questions about Audrey Mosson. I am also very grateful to Mavis Mottershead and Monica Norris for talking to me about their memories of being in the tower children's ballet.

And of course, a big thank you to my family, friends and colleagues for your kind support.

Also available . . .

Susan Brownrigg
KINTANA
and the
CAPTAIN'S
CURSE
From the author of
Gracie Fairshaw and the Mysterious Guest

If you liked this, you'll love . . .

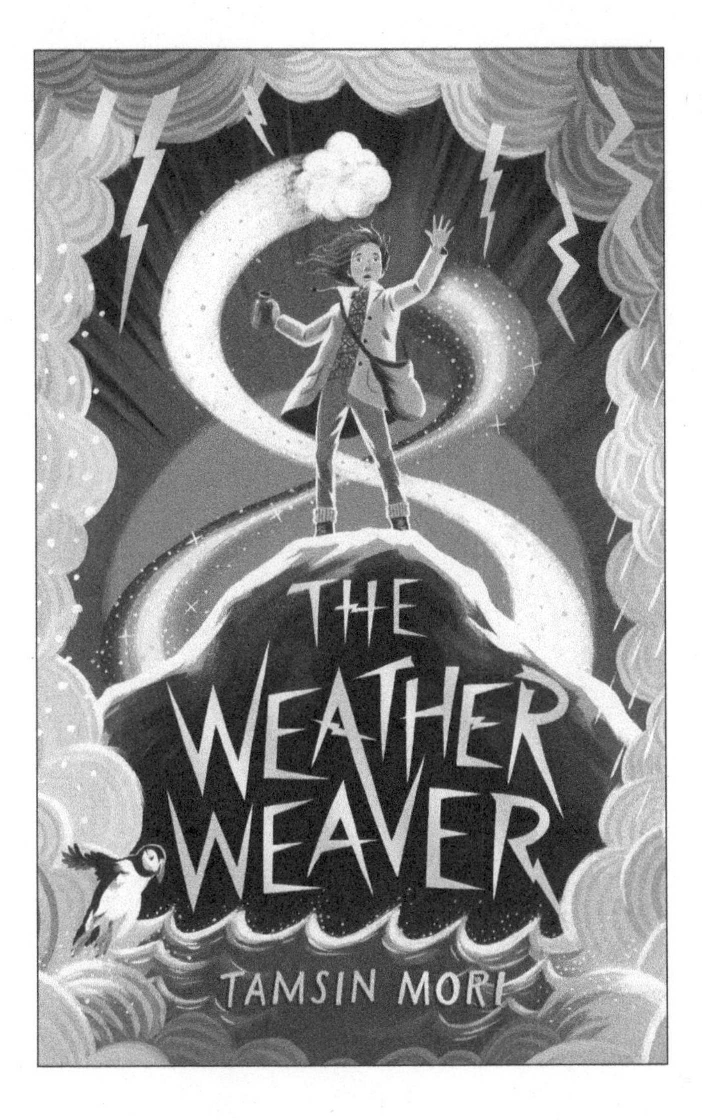
THE
WEATHER
WEAVER
TAMSIN MORI

MEET
MATILDA
ROCKET
BUILDER
WRITTEN BY
DOM CONLON
ILLUSTRATED BY
HEIDI CANNON

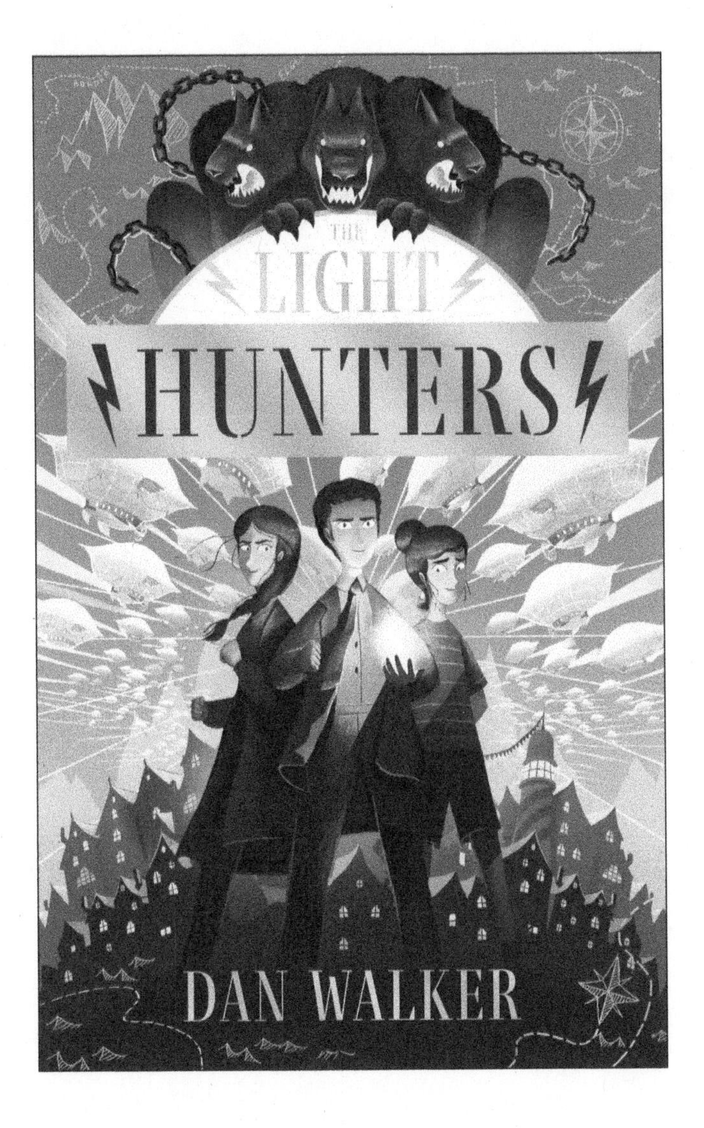
THE
LIGHT
HUNTERS
DAN WALKER

Have you ever wondered how books are made?

UCLan Publishing are based in the North of England and involve BA Publishing and MA Publishing students from the University of Central Lancashire at every stage of the publishing process.

BA Publishing and MA Publishing students work closely alongside our company and work on producing books as part of their course – some of which are selected to be published and printed by UCLan Publishing. Students also gain first-hand experience conceiving and running innovative high-level events to leverage sales, as well as running content creation business enterprises.

Our approach to business and teaching has been recognized academically and within the publishing industry. We have been awarded Best Newcomer at the Independent Publishing Guild Awards (2019) and a *Times* Higher Education Award for Excellence and Innovation in the Arts (2018).

As our business continues to grow, so too does the experience our students have upon entering UCLan Publishing.

To find out more, please visit
www.uclanpublishing.com/courses/